THE WATER WAR

KEVIN MILLER

MILLSTONE
PRESS

Kevin Miller/Millstone Press
Box 380
Kimberley, BC, Canada V1A 2Y9

www.kevinmillerxi.com
www.facebook.com/MilliganCreekSeries

The Water War/Kevin Miller. -- 1st ed.
ISBN: 1727651383

Cover illustration by Kierston Vande Kraats (https://kvdk.carbonmade.com)

Dedication

For Rick and Glenn Larson, Lark Miller, and Kevin Bull

Contents

1

The New Girl

"What'd you say her name was again?"

"Fiona. Fiona Pickleberrybush."

"Pickleberrybush?" Twelve-year-old Matt Taylor pushed back his trademark Edmonton Oilers cap and grinned at his older brother, Chad. Then he turned back to the boy they had pulled aside on Milligan Creek's Main Street. It was practically deserted, shimmering heat waves rising from the asphalt on the hot mid-July day.

The boy, Sheldon Narfuson, was dressed in neon green swim trunks and a T-shirt, a rainbow-striped beach towel slung over his shoulder. He looked around nervously, as if eager to get on his way. "I don't know what kind of name it is," he replied, jingling some loose change in his hand, "but you should see her." He smiled dreamily. "Every guy in town is nuts for her. That's why we're all down at the pool. She's been there every day since she showed up. And here's the crazy thing." He leaned in close, as if sharing an important secret, "she never goes in the water."

"Why not?" Matt asked.

Sheldon shrugged as he hurried down the street. "Why don't you ask her yourself?"

Matt shook his head as he watched Sheldon round the corner toward the pool. Then he turned back to Chad. "Can you believe that? Look at this place; it's a ghost town. And all because of a girl?"

Chad scanned the nearly empty street, which would normally be teeming with kids heading to the arcade, buying ice cream, or just hanging out. All he saw were a few senior citizens sitting on the bench outside the Milligan Creek Co-op, whiling away the afternoon as they swapped stories in the shade. Above them on the side of the store was a billboard advertising Milligan Creek Daze, the community's upcoming annual summer festival, which included a rodeo, a midway, a parade, a softball tournament, and other activities, the most anticipated of which was the crowning of Miss Milligan Creek.

Chad turned back to his brother. "She must be pretty special to get everyone so riled up. Maybe we should head down to the pool and see what all the fuss is about."

Matt scoffed. "Are you kidding me? Go stare at a girl who won't even go in the water? She probably just doesn't want to get her hair wet. Let's stop by Dean's house instead. He's one guy who I can guarantee hasn't fallen under Pickleberrybush's spell. He's probably been sitting in a lawn chair at the end of our driveway for the last two weeks waiting for Joyce to get home."

Joyce was Matt and Chad's older sister. Dean Muller, one of their best friends, had been in love with her for as long as they could remember.

Matt and Chad's family had just returned from a road trip to Vancouver. They left on the last day of school and took their time camping to and from the coast, finally arriving home in mid-July. As much as the boys liked the ocean, they had been restless throughout much of the trip.

The mountains made them feel claustrophobic, and they were only able to relax once they finally descended from the foothills back onto the prairies.

Matt started down the street and then stopped and looked back when he realized Chad was still standing on the corner, gazing longingly toward the pool. "Aren't you coming?" Matt asked.

Chad cast a final glance toward the pool and then turned reluctantly to follow his brother. "I guess so."

"Sheesh," Matt said as Chad caught up to him. "I was starting to think Miss Pickleberrybush was already getting to your brain too."

Five minutes later, Matt's knuckles rapped on a screen door as he and Chad stood on the front porch of Dean's two-story home. Chad swept his hair out of his eyes as they waited for someone to answer, his bangs already sticking to his forehead in the summer heat. "Girl or no girl, hanging out at the pool's not such a bad idea on a day like today."

"Yeah, maybe," Matt said. "But I've got all sorts of other plans for the summer, and we've already lost two weeks to—oh, hi, Mrs. Muller," Matt said as he saw her silhouette appear inside.

Mrs. Muller pushed open the screen door and fanned herself with a newspaper as she looked Matt up and down. "Well, well, well. Matt Taylor. Back already, hey? I was hoping you'd be out of my hair for at least half the summer. Now not only do I have to put up with this heat, I have to put up with you too. Hello, Chad."

Chad grinned. "Hello, Mrs. Muller. Is Dean around?"

She sniffed. "You mean you guys haven't heard? About little Miss Pickleberrybush?"

Matt's jaw dropped. "Not Dean too!"

She nodded. "Yup. Even Andrew's caught the bug."

"Andrew?" Matt and Chad exchanged surprised looks. Andrew Loewen was the brains of the bunch and, to the boys' knowledge, he had yet to show interest in anything other than technology and inventions, never mind girls.

"You should see them all," Mrs. Muller continued. "Jumping off the diving boards, doing push-ups on the pool deck, competing to see who can swim the farthest underwater—anything they can think of to impress her. The funny thing is, she doesn't bat an eye. Just lies there on her beach towel, sunglasses on and headphones over her ears. Probably loving every minute of it."

Matt sighed. "This is depressing."

"Tell me about it," Mrs. Muller said, wiping her forehead. "I haven't been able to get Dean to cut the lawn for a week. Not that I blame him in this heat."

Matt turned to leave. "Well, thanks anyway, Mrs. Muller."

"No problem, boys. If you do see Dean, make sure you tell him: no grass, no cash. And watch out, or Miss Pickleberrybush'll cast her spell on you too!" She laughed as she let the screen door slam shut.

"Not a chance!" Matt retorted as he and Chad headed down the sidewalk. Chad didn't look nearly as sure.

§

"Well, what are we going to do for the rest of the day?" Chad asked a few minutes later as the brothers made their way back downtown.

"I don't know," Matt replied, kicking a rock into the gutter. "Maybe head to the arcade? At least it's air conditioned, and with Miss Pickleberrybush in town, there won't be a line-up at any of the good games."

"I don't know," Chad said, squinting as he watched two men in an articulating hydraulic boom lift repainting the town's water tower, which loomed over Milligan Creek like a bright white lollipop. The bulb at the top of the tower had the town's name printed on it in big black letters. "Seems a waste to spend such a beautiful day inside."

"What else do you suggest?"

The boys stopped where their bikes were parked outside the convenience store on Main Street, and Chad looked longingly toward the pool. Matt smacked himself in the forehead. "Oh no, not my own brother!"

Chad turned back to him. "Come on, Matt, aren't you even a little curious?"

"No!"

"Well, I am." He grabbed his bike out of the rack and got on.

"So, that's it?" Matt asked. "You're abandoning me?"

Chad looked back over his shoulder as he pedaled away. "No one's stopping you. Besides, one little look couldn't hurt."

"Oh yeah? Tell that to all the people who looked at Medusa. They turned to stone!"

"Fiona's not Medusa!" Chad called over his shoulder.

"How do you know?" Matt replied, kicking another stone into the gutter. "She's probably worse."

2

WELCOME TO MILLIGAN CREEK!

The next morning, Matt woke up early, bursting with ideas for the day. He rolled over and was about to say something to Chad, but when he looked across the room, his brother's bed was empty. He listened for a moment and heard the shower running. A quick look at his digital alarm clock told him it was only 7:37. Why was Chad up so early? Then he remembered: the new girl. They'd been home for less than twenty-four hours, and Chad had already lost his mind.

A few minutes later, when Chad crept into their bedroom with a towel around his waist, thinking Matt was still asleep, Matt's nose told him his worst fears had come true.

"Is that . . ." He sat up and sniffed. "Cologne?"

Chad reddened slightly. "Maybe."

"Where'd you get it? And why the heck are you wearing it?"

Chad shrugged. "I figured it was probably time."

Matt frowned. "Time for what?"

"You know, time to—"

Matt leaned closer and squinted in the dim light of the darkened bedroom, dust-filled beams of sunlight just starting to leak past the edges of their window blind. "What's the matter with your face?"

Chad put his hand to where a couple of pieces of toilet paper were stuck to his cheek, a red dot in the middle of each one.

"Were you . . . shaving?"

Chad's face reddened further. "Maybe."

Matt fell back onto his bed, laughing. "Are you kidding me? You don't even have anything to shave."

Chad ran a hand over his face as he looked in the mirror. "Maybe not, but I read somewhere that the more you shave, the faster and thicker it'll grow."

Matt's eyes narrowed in accusation. "You're doing it for her, aren't you?"

Chad lowered his gaze. He knew better than to deny it. Matt shook his head slowly in disappointment. "I can't believe it. You've only seen her once, and you're already head over heels. You're worse than Dean."

Chad looked up, his body stiffening. "You haven't seen her, Matt. If you did—"

"I don't need to see her. All I have to see is the way she's affecting everyone else. It's pathetic."

Chad opened his dresser drawer and pulled out some clothes. Matt sat up and swung his legs over the edge of his bed as his brother got dressed. "Where are you off to in such a hurry, anyway?"

"Where do you think?"

Matt looked at the clock. "You're kidding me, right? The pool doesn't even open until nine."

Chad stuffed his swimsuit and a beach towel into his backpack. "I'm going to line up early to make sure I get a good spot."

"A good spot? A good spot for what?"

Chad slung his backpack over his shoulder and looked

at Matt. "What do you think? You're welcome to come down any time you like, Matt. All the guys are asking about you."

"Well, if they want me, they know exactly where they can find me. And it won't be anywhere near that stupid pool—or Fiona Pickleberrybush." Matt fell back onto his bed with a thump.

Chad took a final look at his brother, as if he felt sorry for him. "Suit yourself," he said. Then he was out the door.

§

A couple of hours later, Matt was slouched in a bucket seat inside the reclaimed MD 500 Defender helicopter fuselage, complete with round bubble windshield, that formed the central part of their tree house. The rest of the structure was made from a hodgepodge of salvaged wood, old windows, and a metal roof. It was an ongoing construction project, the boys constantly adding new features, including bunk beds, bookshelves, a mini fridge, shutters, and window boxes full of flowers, which were Dean's pet project. However, Matt noticed the flowers looked wilted and neglected, likely another casualty of the other boys' ongoing fascination with Fiona. The bubble windshield was also in need of a good cleaning, but Matt didn't have the heart to do it.

He had just picked up a duck decoy they had carved as part of a previous adventure when the tree house began to shake, a sure sign someone was climbing the ladder.

"Finally," Matt said, setting the decoy on the table. "I knew those guys would come to their senses sooner or later."

However, when the trap door flipped open, Matt gaped in surprise. "Joyce? What are you doing here?"

"Don't look so shocked," Joyce said as she climbed inside. "Can't I come out and visit my own brother?"

"Of course, but—"

"You don't have to explain. I know *all* about it."

Matt leaned forward, sensing an ally against the new force of evil that had entered their small town. "You've heard about her? Fiona?"

Joyce nodded as she slumped into a bucket seat. "I haven't just heard about her, I've seen her. Primping and preening and tossing her hair. You think the *guys* are going nuts over her? You should see the girls. They can't stand the fact that Fiona is getting all the attention, so they're falling over themselves trying to get it back. Even worse, they're turning on each other. It's a total cat fight, and it's embarrassing to watch. I can't imagine what will happen if she enters the Miss Milligan Creek contest. The other girls will tear their eyes out just to get a shot at second place. Anyway, I couldn't take it anymore, which is why I'm here. I hate to say it, Matt, but you may be our only hope. You've got to do something."

Matt raised his eyebrows. "Me? What can I do?"

Joyce threw her hands up in exasperation. "I don't know. What you always do. Something outrageous. Annoying. Something—anything—to draw people's attention away from her."

Matt sat back in silence for a few moments, his mind racing. Then he sprang to his feet. "That's it!" he said, already heading toward the trap door. "This town needs to see Miss Pickleberrybush as the monster she really is, and I know just where to do it!"

§

As Matt approached the pool, a large outdoor facility, complete with high and low diving boards and a paddling pool for young children, he heard the typical sounds one might hear from such a place on a hot summer day: kids yelling and laughing, splashing, and the pounding of the diving boards as people bounced on them and then dove into the water. It sounded like just another day at the pool; however, Matt knew it was anything but.

He walked up to the chain-link fence that surrounded the pool and looked inside. The place was packed. He saw a few families with small children, but almost everyone else was Matt's age and older—pre-teens and younger teenagers. Most of the guys were lined up waiting to get on one of the diving boards. Some of them were clearly flexing as they waited their turn, others were rubbing on sunscreen, and some were even doing push-ups on the pool deck, just like Mrs. Muller had described. As for the girls, many of them had donned sunglasses and were wearing Walkman headphones as they lay suntanning on their towels, all of them trying to be just like Fiona. How pathetic!

Just then, Matt spotted Dean at the top of the high-diving board. As far as Matt could remember, he had never seen Dean that high up before, never mind on a diving board. As Dean edged toward the end of the board, he looked down at a cluster of teenagers on the pool deck. Matt realized Fiona had to be somewhere in the midst of that crowd. He stood on his tiptoes to catch a glimpse of her, but he couldn't see over everyone else's heads.

"C'mon, Dean, we don't have all day!" one of the boys in line yelled, crossing his arms over his chest to keep himself warm in the breeze.

"Yeah, c'mon, Dean!" another boy said. "Dea-nie! Dea-nie!" The chant was picked up by the rest of the group, and suddenly, everyone at the pool was calling Dean's name.

His freckled cheeks pasty white and his eyes as big as

Toonies, Dean swallowed hard as he stared down at the water. Then he steeled himself, raised his arms over his head like an Olympic diver, took one quick step forward with his left foot, drove his right knee up, came down hard on two feet, and launched himself into the air.

At first, Matt was impressed. He had no idea Dean knew how to dive. But as Dean's body arced up, reaching the point that would have led to a graceful swan dive, it kept on going—and going—until Dean's legs went over his head, and he tilted into more of a laid-out front flip. It might have worked too, if Dean hadn't panicked. But he did panic, legs and arms flailing, his face a mask of terror as he strove to halt his rotation. He tried to call for help, but it came out more like "Helgrhhaahh!" A moment later, a terrible smack shattered the serene summer day, followed by an anguished silence.

All eyes were on the pool, lifeguards at the ready in case Dean failed to come back up. When he did surface, his face was red, but that was nothing compared to his back, which was glowing like a stoplight.

"Did she . . . did she see it?" Dean croaked as the two lifeguards—one rippling with muscles and the other pale and thin—hauled him out of the water and laid him on the pool deck.

"Excuse me?" Waldo, the burly lifeguard, asked, hardly believing his ears considering the trauma Dean had just experienced.

"F-Fiona," Dean said. "D-did she see my dive?"

Everyone—including the lifeguards—swiveled toward the gaggle of kids surrounding Fiona and then turned back to Dean.

"Forget about her," the skinny lifeguard, Lance, replied. "How many fingers am I holding up?"

Dean stared at him with bleary eyes. "You're holding up . . . f-fingers?"

18

Matt smacked himself in the forehead. That did it. This had gone way too far. The guys' infatuation with Fiona was going to get someone killed if he didn't do something, and quickly. But what?

His racing mind stopped when he spotted a grey fire hose lying on the pool deck. Having only been turned on partway, it was shooting a gentle stream of water into the paddling pool to refill it. Matt looked from the hose to the cluster of people around Fiona . . . and grinned.

§

Minutes later, everything at the pool was back to normal—guys doing tricks off the diving boards, girls doing their best to strike alluring poses as they suntanned, and Fiona, flat on her back on the pool deck, sunglasses and Walkman headphones on, seemingly unaware of it all.

Suddenly, a scream went up, and the crowd parted like the Red Sea, people tripping over each other in their haste to get out of the way. Others turned to see what the fuss was about. Their eyes were met by Matt, who was lugging the fire hose. Having turned it up all the way, the hose was bucking and vibrating in his hands, just waiting to unleash a torrent of water once Matt flicked the lever forward.

Across the pool, Waldo and Lance sprang to their feet from where they had been tending to Dean. "Hey!" Waldo yelled. "Put that thing down!"

Matt continued his advance, undaunted. "Hey, Fiona!" he yelled. "Yeah, I'm talking to you, Miss Pickleberrybush!"

Their eyes wide with horror, everyone turned to Fiona, who continued to lie on her back, unmoving.

"Get him!" Waldo yelled, and then he ran one way around the pool while Lance ran the other.

Dean lifted his head weakly. "Hey, w-what about me?"

"I know you can hear me," Matt continued, every head swiveling back toward him. "I hear no one's given you a proper welcome to Milligan Creek, so I thought I'd do the honors."

"Matt, no!" Chad stepped out of the crowd with his hands raised, Andrew beside him. Both boys planted themselves firmly between the fire hose and Fiona. Other gallant gentlemen stepped forward to do the same.

"Out of the way, Chad," Matt said, his grip tightening on the hose, "and prepare to see Miss Pickleberrybush for who she really is."

Chad shook his head firmly and crossed his arms. "I can't let you do this, Matt."

Matt shrugged. "To quote my older, 'wiser' sibling, 'Suit yourself.'" He grabbed the lever. "Fiona, prepare to get your hair wet!"

"Don't you dare!" Lance yelled as he and Waldo closed in.

With no time to lose, Matt jammed the lever forward, and a jet of water shot out of the hose. But instead of hitting Chad and Andrew or Fiona, it shot straight up into the air, the force of it knocking Matt backwards. He struggled to control the bucking fire hose, stumbled a few steps, and then fell flat on his back into the paddling pool, the fire hose flying out of his hands.

People screamed and backed away, shielding themselves with their hands and their beach towels as the fire hose whipped across the pool deck like an angry, dying snake, water spraying everywhere. Another scream went up as the crowd's momentum forced many of them to fall into the pool like a herd of lemmings.

The two lifeguards converged on the fire hose and wrestled it to the deck. Waldo finally got his hand on the lever and turned it off. A cry of relief went up from the crowd, and then every eye turned to a group of guys who had formed a protective circle around Fiona, shielding her with towels, beach umbrellas, and their bodies, all of them dripping wet. When the crowd parted, there was Fiona, still lying flat on her back, sunglasses and headphones on, not a drop of water on her, seemingly unaware of the events that had just transpired.

In the paddling pool, Matt spluttered and splashed as he struggled to stand up in the knee-deep water.

"Matt Taylor!" Waldo bellowed as he marched toward him. "You are hereby—"

"I know, I know, banned from the pool," Matt said as he climbed back onto the deck.

"Indefinitely," Lance added as he took one of Matt's arms and Waldo took the other.

As they marched Matt toward the gate, he looked back over his shoulder, his eyes blazing with defiance. "You haven't heard the last of me, Fiona Pickleberrybush!"

Everyone turned toward Fiona, eager for her response, but nothing came. Only when they turned away did a ghost of a smile cross her lips.

3

A SURPRISE VISITOR

The next morning found Matt all alone in the tree house once again, sulking at his banishment from the pool and, more importantly, his public humiliation at the hands of Fiona Pickleberrybush. She was fast becoming his archenemy, even though they had never met. And despite the previous day's stunt, he wasn't even sure if she knew he existed.

A vibration in the floor told him someone was climbing the ladder. He sighed heavily. "If it's all the same to you, Joyce, I'd really rather be alone right—"

His words were interrupted when the trap door flew open, revealing not Joyce but Chad. He was followed by Andrew and Dean, who grimaced as he clambered inside, his back still smarting from his high-dive stunt the day before.

Matt checked his watch dramatically and then crossed his arms. "Shouldn't you guys be staking out a spot at the pool right about now?"

The other guys were silent as they each claimed a bucket seat around the table. Dean winced as he grasped the arms of his chair and slowly lowered himself into a sitting position. The other boys remained quiet, their eyes downcast as Matt glared at each one in turn. "What's the matter?" he asked finally. "Did you guys get kicked out of the pool too?"

Chad was the first to meet his brother's gaze, his face serious. "That was a stupid stunt you pulled yesterday, Matt."

Matt's eyes flashed with anger. "Stupid? You think what I did was stupid? What about all you—"

"But it was the wake-up call we needed," Chad continued. "All of us. If you hadn't of done that, who knows? We might have wasted the entire summer waiting around on the pool deck for Fiona to acknowledge us."

Matt looked at Andrew, who nodded silently, and Dean, whose face contorted with pain as he shifted in his seat to ease the pressure on his back. He looked at Matt with pleading eyes. "Do you . . . do you think Joyce can ever forgive me?"

"No," Matt said. "Definitely not."

Dean's face fell. Matt turned to his brother. "So, does this mean all the guys have come to their senses?"

Chad shook his head. "Nope. Just us."

"And the girls?"

"Still there. Still preening. Still doing everything they can to draw attention away from Fiona."

Matt pushed his chair back from the table. "So, that's it then. This summer is officially ruined."

"Not necessarily," Andrew replied.

Matt gave him a skeptical look. "Oh yeah? Why not?"

"Because as stupid as your stunt was," Chad said, "it gave us an idea."

"Something to draw the guys—and the girls—away from the pool," Andrew added.

"Oh really." Matt leaned back in his chair and put his hands behind his head. "I can't wait to hear it."

Chad looked at Andrew and nodded. In response, Andrew unfolded a piece of newspaper and slid it across the table. "I stumbled upon this when you guys were away. I meant to show it to you when you and Chad got back, but I kind of got . . . distracted."

"I'll say." Matt grabbed it and read the headline out loud. "Spy versus spy: you can shoot or die." It featured a photo of a guy with a suction-cup dart gun held to his head. Matt grinned at the other boys. "You're suggesting we assassinate her? I like the sound of this idea already."

Chad sighed. "Just read the article."

Matt was silent for a few moments as he scanned the story. When he was finished, he looked up at the other guys. "This is brilliant."

"Isn't it cool?" Chad replied. "It's called Assassin, a game where every player is both a killer *and* a target."

"And the last person standing," Dean paused and grimaced as he shifted in his chair, "wins the prize."

"There's just one problem," Matt said, tossing the article onto the table. "Who's going to play?"

Andrew frowned. "What do you mean?"

"What I mean is, everyone is glued to the pool deck twenty-four seven doing their darnedest to impress Miss Tickleberrybush—"

"Pickleberrybush."

"Whatever. My point is, no one's gonna want to leave to play the game."

The other boys fell silent once again and exchanged guilty looks. Matt's forehead creased as he realized something was up. "What's going on?"

"Well, we may have found a way to solve that problem," Chad said. He nodded at Andrew, who thumped his foot on the floor three times. In response, the tree house began to shudder as someone ascended the ladder.

"Let me guess," Matt said, grinning as he waited for

25

the surprise visitor to appear, "you're going to make the grand prize a kiss from Joyce."

Chad exchanged a look with Andrew and then turned back to Matt. "Surprisingly close."

"That would have been a great idea!" Dean said, his face lighting up.

"Not if you're her brother," Chad replied.

"Oh yeah." Dean's smile faded as quickly as it had appeared.

Matt raised one eyebrow. "Seriously? You think a kiss from Joyce is going to make guys want to play?"

"Maybe not that, but this might." Chad got up and walked over to the trapdoor. When he flipped it open, Matt sprang out of his chair in shock. Standing before him—sunglasses, Walkman headphones, and all—was the one, the only, Fiona Pickleberrybush.

4

THIS MEANS WAR

"You . . . you can't be in here!" Matt stammered.

"Why not?" Andrew asked.

"Because she's . . . she's a girl!"

"What about Joyce?" Dean protested.

"That's different!"

Matt stumbled back as Fiona accepted Chad's offer of a helping hand and climbed into the tree house, the trapdoor slamming shut behind her.

All four boys stared in silence as Fiona paused to look around, taking in every detail. Finally, she nodded and pulled off her headphones, letting them hang around her neck. "Nice place," she said. Immediately, Chad, Andrew, and Dean let out a sigh of relief, none of them realizing they had been holding their breath, anxiously awaiting her approval.

Having examined the tree house, Fiona turned her attention to Matt. "Well, well, well, if it isn't Milligan Creek's resident fireman."

Matt's face reddened. "Fire . . . what? How did you—"

Fiona tapped her sunglasses. "I may wear sunglasses, but I'm not blind."

Dean leaned in close to Matt and held his hand to

the side of his mouth. "She even wears them at night," he stage-whispered. "Sensitive eyes."

Matt scoffed. "Yeah, right."

The room descended back into an uncomfortable silence until Fiona gestured toward the bucket seats. "May I?"

"By all means." Chad hastened out of the way and gestured for Fiona to take his chair.

Matt scowled. "Where are *you* going to sit, Chad?"

"It's alright; I can sit on a stool," Chad replied, grabbing a barstool from under the window.

"But—"

"I said it's alright, Matt. Fiona's our *guest*. Try to show some manners."

The other boys settled uneasily into their chairs, Matt being the last to do so. "I still don't understand what's going on," he said. "What's *she* got to do with the game?"

"I'm right in front of you, you know," Fiona said. "You can talk to me directly."

Matt glanced at her and then looked away. "I'm sorry, but I can't talk to anyone who wears sunglasses indoors."

Fiona chuckled, and then the room lapsed into another uneasy silence.

"Does somebody want to explain what's going on?" Matt asked finally.

Chad cleared his throat. "After the fire hose incident yesterday, for which I think you owe Fiona an apology, by the way." He gave his brother a meaningful look.

Matt looked up in surprise and then scowled at the table, crossing his arms. "Sorry."

Fiona smiled sweetly. "Don't mention it."

"Anyway," Chad continued, "I did some asking around and realized everyone had been so busy ogling Fiona or trying to impress her on the diving boards that no one had actually gone up and introduced themselves. So, that's what I did. And I'm glad too, because Fiona was starting to think she had moved to a town full of weirdos."

"I'm still not totally convinced I haven't," Fiona said, a thin smile teasing her lips.

"Hmph." Matt squeezed his arms even harder around his chest. "At least we don't wear sunglasses and headphones around the clock."

Fiona arched her left eyebrow. "But for some reason, you think the best way to welcome a new girl to town is to blast her with a fire hose."

That got a chuckle out of Andrew and Dean, until Matt silenced them with a glare.

"Once I actually talked to Fiona," Chad said, "I realized she was just as worried about having a boring summer as we were. When Andrew told me about the Assassin game, I put two and two together, and here we are."

"Wait a second," Matt said, shaking his head. "Two plus two? How does that equal Fiona?"

"Simple," Andrew replied. "We realized that if we could convince Fiona to play the game, everyone else would follow her."

Matt turned to Fiona. "And why would *you* want to play Assassin?"

Fiona shrugged. "I'm bored. Besides, I hear there's going to be a cash prize, and I plan to win."

Matt's eyes flew to his brother. "A cash prize? What are you going to do, break open your piggy bank?"

"Not just me, dummy," Chad said. "We all are. There's going to be an entry fee, and we'll run it like a fifty-fifty draw. Half the money will go to covering the cost of running the game, and the other half will go to the winner."

"How much money are we talking about?"

Chad turned to Andrew, who shrugged. "It all depends on how many people play," he said. "We're thinking ten bucks a head. If we can get fifty players, that'll be two hundred and fifty bucks for the winner."

"And if a guy wins, we thought we'd sweeten the pot," Chad added.

Matt looked at him. "Oh yeah, how?"

Dean smiled, answering before Chad could. "The winner gets to go on a date with Fiona!"

Matt's nostrils flared as he looked at the interloper. "A date? With Fiona? What happens if a girl wins?"

"Simple," Chad replied, grinning at the other boys. "If a girl wins, she gets to go on a date . . . with you."

Matt looked at Fiona in horror. "With me? But that means if I win, I have to . . . and if she wins . . .."

Smiling, Fiona turned to Matt. "I like Chinese food, if and when it comes to it."

Matt scoffed. "Then I'll tell you your fortune cookie message in advance: quit while you're ahead!"

5

THE RULES

Two days later, a lineup of kids extended out the side door of Dean's garage and onto the sidewalk, their shadows stretching across the cement in the orange early evening light. It hadn't taken long to get the word out about the game. Most of the kids were still hanging out at the pool, and the moment they heard Fiona was playing, the sign-up rate was almost 100 percent, with players begging for or borrowing money from their siblings and parents or collecting enough cans and bottles to pay the ten-dollar entry fee.

Dean looked around nervously as he and Matt headed inside. "I still don't understand why we had to have the meeting at my place. My parents will kill me if they find out I had all these people over without permission."

"Relax," Matt said, clapping his hand on Dean's shoulder. "We'd do it at our place, but we live too far out of town. Besides, it's only your garage, not your house, and your parents won't be back from the lake until tomorrow night."

"Or so you think. I wouldn't put it past them to show up early, just to test me."

"You worry way too much."

"You would too if you had my parents."

Matt grinned. "You have a point."

Dean groaned. "That's not very reassuring." He took one last look around before he followed Matt into his family's detached garage. The structure was larger than a typical garage, more like a workshop, seeing as it also served as the headquarters for the electronics business owned and operated by Dean's dad.

Inside, Chad and Joyce sat behind a card table as participants filled out registration forms for the game. "Once you've signed in and paid your fee, go over to Andrew, and he'll take your picture," Chad said. As if on cue, the garage was illuminated by a flash from a Polaroid camera, followed by a whir as the camera spewed out a fresh print, which Andrew shook vigorously to speed up the development process.

A swarthy boy with beads of sweat forming on his upper lip eyed the fat Mason jar beside Chad. It was already bursting with crumpled ten-dollar bills. "That's a lot of money in there. What's to say you guys aren't just going to run off and blow it all at the arcade?"

Joyce's eyes bored into him. "Seriously, Joey?"

He shrugged. "You have to admit it's tempting."

"If you don't trust us, you don't have to play," Joyce said, snatching the registration form from him.

"And miss out on an opportunity for a date with Fiona? Not a chance." Joey grabbed it back and picked up a pen. "She is playing, right?" He looked around the garage, where numerous kids who had already registered were chatting and milling about, but Fiona was nowhere to be seen.

"Of course," Chad said.

"Then where is she?"

"She'll be here."

Joey crossed his arms and stared at Chad. "When?"

"Soon!"

Finally, Joey fished a ten-dollar bill out of his pocket and stuffed it into the jar. "She'd better be, or I'm asking for a refund."

As Joey filled out his form, Chad looked at Joyce and tapped his left wrist. "Where is she?" he mouthed. Joyce shrugged and then smiled at the next prospective player as she handed her a registration form.

"Here you go," Joyce said. "We need your name, address, and phone number . . .."

§

Thirty minutes later, everyone had registered, but there was still no sign of Fiona. The garage was packed with kids. They were getting hot—and restless.

"It's like a sauna in here!" someone said. "Can't we open the overhead door?"

"No!" Dean cried, covering the button with his hand before someone could press it.

"Why not?" another kid asked.

"This meeting is top secret," Matt said, stepping forward. "That's one of the first rules of the game: kids only. If our parents find out we're playing a game that involves assassinating each other, even if we're only pretending to do it, they'll shut us down. That means anyone who spills the beans is automatically disquali—"

Matt stopped short when he realized no one was listening to him, their eyes drawn to the garage's side door. He followed their gaze and realized why. "It's about time," he muttered as Fiona made her entrance.

She removed her headphones and smiled. "Sorry I'm late."

"Not a problem," Matt said, clenching his teeth in frustration as the crowd parted to make way for the guest of honor.

"Can we get a fan over here?" someone yelled. Moments later, as if by magic, someone produced a desktop fan, aimed it at Fiona, and turned it on. Her hair blowing in the breeze and made translucent by the overhead light, she looked as if she was on the set of a fashion shoot rather than inside a garage full of sweaty kids. The surrounding boys stared at her in wonder, their faces illuminated by goofy grins, completely unaware of their own discomfort as they basked in the glow of Fiona's glory.

She nodded her thanks to Joey, who had set up the fan. His round cheeks glowed the color of ripe McIntosh apples. Then she turned to Matt. "Please, don't mind me, Matthew. Continue."

Matt cleared his throat to suppress his irritation. "It's Matt, thank you very much. Anyway, as I was saying, this game is for kids only. No adults can play, and no adults can know about it."

A hand shot up. "Why not?"

"Because that makes it harder—and more fun," Chad replied. "And remember, we don't want them to shut us down."

Matt nodded in agreement. "Exactly. Apart from that, the basic rules are simple. Each player is both predator and prey. If you're smart, you'll keep the person you're going after a secret. No place is off limits, not even your victim's home. If you get killed, you're out of the game, and you have to surrender your target to whoever takes you out. Then the person who killed you goes after your victim and so on and so on. The last person standing is the winner."

Another hand went up. "How do we prove that we killed someone?"

"With these." Andrew held up a piece of paper with

a picture of Donald Duck on it. "In your assassin package—along with a water gun, a photo of your victim, and information about where your victim lives—each player will receive a custom page from a paint-with-water coloring book. As you can see," he paused and shot the paper with a water gun, "if this paper gets wet, it turns color." Sure enough, as the water dripped down the page, it bled colors with it. "This target must be worn on the outside of your clothing at all times."

"What if we accidentally get it wet?" someone asked.

"Then you're out of the game," Andrew said. "Whoever is hunting you gets a free kill, and you have to surrender your gun and your victim's information to headquarters. So, whatever you do, protect this little piece of paper at all costs, because each one is unique, and there are no replacements."

"Where's headquarters?" Joey asked.

"Right here," Matt said, pointing at the floor.

Dean looked at him in horror. "What?"

Matt motioned for Dean to zip it. "We'll talk about it later," he whispered. Then he turned back to the group. "This is a safe zone. No one can be assassinated inside this building."

"Can we kill someone who's trying to kill us?" a tall girl asked.

"No," Matt said shaking his head. "You can only kill your target. If someone's coming after you, all you can do is run—unless that person also happens to be your target."

"So, that's it?" another girl said. "Once we get killed, we're out of the game? That's pretty boring for the people who get taken out first."

The comment was met by murmurs of agreement.

"That's where the game gets interesting," Chad said. "Every time you take someone out, you get a bonus: either something to help defend you, such as an umbrella, or something to help you attack, such as a better weapon. Or, if you choose, you can bring a 'dead' player back into the game. That player will be issued a new target to go on their chest. Then he or she can help you go after your victim. If the dead player gets killed again, they're out until someone else brings them back in. And remember: if you bring people onto your team, you'll have to split the prize money with them. How you work that out is up to you."

"How will we know who's on whose team?" another kid asked.

"With these," Joyce said, stepping forward in a pair of sunglasses with pink neon frames.

"Wow, we'll look just like Fiona!" a girl said.

"Do we have to wear pink ones?" Billy asked.

"No," Joyce replied, taking off her sunglasses and holding up a half dozen pairs of sunglasses in various colors. "Each team will get a different color."

Another boy raised his hand. "Who's going to oversee all this to make sure everyone plays by the rules?"

Joyce pointed her thumb at her chest. "I am." She crossed her arms and scowled at the crowd of sweaty faces. "Any more questions?"

"Yeah, is the part about the date with Fiona true?" Joey asked, his bright eyes filled with hope.

Everyone turned toward Miss Pickleberrybush, who was still basking in the breeze created by the fan while everyone around her dripped with sweat.

"Of course," Joyce said. "The same goes for the date with Matt."

Another girl put up her hand. "If we win, do we have to go on a date with Matt?"

Matt gasped in wounded surprise, but Joyce smiled. "No, the date is completely optional," she said. "Any more questions?"

"Moo."

Everyone turned toward the sound. They knew it could only have come from one person. "Yes, Ben?" Matt asked.

"Are we allowed to tell cows about the game?" Ben Somerville had been obsessed with cows for as long as anyone could remember.

Matt shared an amused look with Chad and Joyce, both of whom struggled to suppress a smile, and then turned back to Ben. "I suppose so."

"Can cows play the game?"

"Excuse me?"

"Can I use a cow to help me assassinate someone?"

Confused, Matt looked to his siblings for support. "I don't know, I—"

"I'm sure we can work something out," Joyce replied. "Talk to me after the meeting. Any more questions?"

When none came, she clapped her hands. "All right then. Make sure you pick up your victim's information package on the way out. And remember: the game starts at midnight tonight, so be sure to—"

She paused as a strange sound rumbled through the garage. Everyone looked around in confusion. Then Dean's eyes flew to the button for the overhead door. "Who pressed it? Who pressed the button?"

"No one!" a boy standing next to it said, holding his hands up to proclaim his innocence. "I was looking at it the entire time."

"Then who . . .." Dean's face went white as the rising door revealed the shape of a middle-aged woman silhouetted in the setting sun. There was no mistaking it.

It was Dean's mother.

6

AN UNEXPECTED PLAYER

The crowd fell silent as Mrs. Muller stepped inside the garage, no one even daring to raise a hand to wipe the sweat streaming down their face. "Well, well, well, what have we here?" She paused and sniffed. "Whew, this place smells like a barn. Why did you have the doors closed?" She looked around. "And where's my son?"

The silent crowd parted, creating a clear path between Mrs. Muller and Dean, whose eyes were on the floor. "We had the doors closed, because we wanted to keep our meeting a secret," he said.

Mrs. Muller crossed her arms and tapped her foot. "A secret, hey? So, I was right to ignore my husband, who decided to spend an extra day fishing, and listen to that little voice in my head telling me to come home from the lake one day early. Care to explain what's going on?"

"It was my idea, Mrs. Muller," Matt said, stepping forward to cover for his friend.

"I didn't ask who," she replied, raising her hand, palm out, to stop Matt from continuing. She fixed her eyes on Dean. "I already knew your name would be mixed up in this somehow, Matt Taylor. I asked *what*. And I was talking to *him*." She pointed at her son.

"We're . . . we're planning a game," Dean said.

Mrs. Muller's eyes narrowed. "A game? What kind of game?"

Dean looked at Matt, who looked at Chad, Andrew, and Joyce, all of them wondering how they should reply.

"It's called Assassin," Joey said before any of them could answer. "Each player is an assassin and a target, and the last person who survives wins."

"We can even use cows," Ben added. "Moo."

Mrs. Muller's eyes narrowed. "You're planning to kill people, in my garage?"

"It's just pretend," Dean said.

Mrs. Muller scoffed. "You think I don't know that?"

"No, but—"

"How do you 'kill' people in this game?"

"With this." Andrew walked forward and held out a water pistol.

Mrs. Muller took it and hefted it in her hand. "What happens when you take out your victim?"

"You get that person's victim," Andrew explained. "And so on and so on until only one person is left."

"And each time you kill someone, you get a better weapon, something you can use to defend yourself, or the chance to bring a 'dead' player back into the game to help you," Matt added, encouraged by the fact that Mrs. Muller seemed more curious than angry.

"And what do you get if you win?"

"Two hundred and fifty dollars," Chad said. "Cash."

Mrs. Muller looked up from the water pistol. "Two hundred and fifty dollars? That's a lot of money. Where'd it come from?"

Joyce held up the Mason jar. "We charged an entrance fee."

Dean's mother nodded slowly as she scanned the

crowd, the kids too afraid to meet her gaze, most of them staring at the floor or nervously eyeing the water gun.

"Don't forget the date," Joey added.

"Date?" Mrs. Muller asked, her interest deepening. "What date?"

"If a boy wins, he gets to go on a date with Fiona," Chad said, pointing at her.

Mrs. Muller smiled. "Ah, Miss Pickleberrybush, I've heard a lot about you." Fiona grinned and gave a small wave. Then Dean's mother turned back to Chad. "And if a girl wins?"

Chad put his arm around Matt. "They get to go on a date . . . with my little brother." He gave Matt's shoulders a squeeze.

"That part's totally optional!" a girl called out.

"Sheesh!" Matt said, pushing Chad away and turning toward the voice. "Do you have to keep mentioning that?"

"Interesting . . .." Mrs. Muller walked slowly toward the Taylor boys, the crowd edging back with every step she took. "A chance to assassinate Matt Taylor or go on a date with him. That sounds too good to pass up. How much was that entry fee again?"

Matt, Chad, Andrew, Dean, and Joyce all exchanged an uncomfortable look. "Uh, no disrespect, Mrs. Muller," Joyce said, "but this game is supposed to be for kids only. That's why we were trying to keep it a secret."

"Don't worry about that," Mrs. Muller said, pulling two five-dollar bills out of her pocket and stuffing it into the Mason jar. "Your secret is safe with me. As for the rest of you . . .." The kids ducked instinctively as she raised the water pistol with both hands and swung it around the garage, as if in search of a target. "You should ask yourself one question . . . do you feel lucky? Pow! Pow! Pow!"

A few girls screamed as Mrs. Muller pretended to

41

shoot, laughing as the kids scrambled out of the way.

Matt nudged his sister. "Can't we just tell her it's too late to fit her in?" he whispered.

"Are you kidding me?" Joyce asked. "This'll make it way more fun." She turned back to Mrs. Muller. "If you'll come this way, we need to take your picture and have you fill out an entry form."

"Gladly," Mrs. Muller said, offering the gun to Matt.

"Keep it," he said. "You're going to need it."

"Oh, so that's how it's going to be, hey?" She flashed a wicked grin. "Just you wait, Matt Taylor." She jabbed him in the chest with the muzzle of her water pistol to emphasize each word. "Just . . . you . . . wait. By the way, I hope you like sushi, because that's what we're going to eat on our date." On that note, she went with Joyce to complete her registration.

Matt shook his head as he watched Mrs. Muller walk away and then turned to address the group. "Okay, people, you heard Joyce. Pick up your victim's information package before you leave. The game starts at midnight. Remember, keep your target dry and your eyes peeled! Good luck!"

As the crowd melted away, Dean stood alone in stunned silence in the middle of the garage, staring at the grease-stained cement floor. "I knew we shouldn't have held the meeting here."

"Relax," Matt said as he approached. "At least she isn't mad at you. However . . .."

Dean peered up at him. "What?"

Matt smiled and leaned in close. "If I were you, I'd sleep with one eye open tonight."

"What do you mean?"

"What if you're her first victim?"

Dean swallowed hard, the blood rushing to his face. "No, Joyce would never—"

"After that stunt you pulled on the diving board to get little Miss Huckleberrybush's attention? Oh yes, she would."

"It's Pickleberrybush," Chad said, approaching them. "And Dean's not the only one who should be sleeping with one eye open tonight—and for many nights to come."

Matt looked at him. "What do you—"

Chad held up his victim's information package and grinned. "I'm not saying my first victim is you, but then again, I'm not saying it isn't."

Matt took an involuntary step back. "My own brother? But—that's it, I'm locking myself in the bathroom for the night. Until the end of the game, if necessary."

Chad laughed. "Have fun explaining that one to Mom and Dad."

"I think it's probably best if none of us hang out together for a while," Andrew said as he joined the group, registration package in hand. "Just in case."

"But this game was supposed to bring us all back together," Matt complained, "not split us apart."

Andrew shrugged. "It will. Eventually, but some of us are going to have to 'die' first."

Matt sighed. "I knew Pickleberrybush would ruin this somehow." He held out his fist to the others. "Well, may the best man win."

The other boys took turns bumping fists with him. "May the best man win," they repeated.

Suddenly, another fist thrust itself into the middle of the group. "Or the best woman."

Matt looked up in surprise. The fist belonged to Fiona. She grinned at him from behind her sunglasses as she waited for him to bump her fist. Instead, he withdrew his hand and pointed at her. "In the words of Dean's mom," he said, jabbing his index finger in the air to emphasize each syllable, "just . . . you . . . wait."

7

THE FIRST CASUALTIES

The following morning promised to be the start of a perfect summer day. The sky was clear, birds were chirping, and hardly a breath of wind rippled the lush green leaves of the towering elm trees that arched gracefully over Milligan Creek's strangely quiet streets. Their thick boughs cast long shadows over the frost-heaved sidewalks, where grass and dandelions struggled to eke out an existence between the cracks in the grey cement slabs.

Down at the pool, lifeguards Waldo and Lance went about their morning routine: cleaning the pool deck, checking the chemical balance in the water, stocking the vending machines, and otherwise preparing for what they assumed would be another busy day. But when the time to open arrived, instead of the usual lineup of rowdy boys and preening girls they had faced ever since Fiona had moved to town, the only people waiting to get in were a mother and her two impatient preschool-age children.

As Waldo opened the door to let them in, he checked his watch. It barely fit around his abnormally thick wrist, which was pumped up due to hours spent in the weight room in preparation for summer days spent flexing and perfecting his tan as he patrolled the pool deck, the picture of anatomical perfection. "That's strange," he said. "Where is everybody?"

Lance, who had just emerged from the ladies' change room with a mop and a bucket, turned the sign on the change room door from "Closed" to "Open." He shrugged. "Beats me, but after all we've been through with Miss Pickleberrybush, you won't find me complaining about a slow day."

"Tell me about it," Waldo said, flexing his right bicep and comparing it to his left while looking at his reflection in the window. "I might even get a bit of time to pump some iron. Even these guns out."

Lance rolled his eyes as he pushed the mop and bucket toward the storage room. "Just don't shoot yourself in the foot, cowboy," he muttered.

"What was that?" Waldo asked, his eyes still glued to his reflection.

"Nothing!" Lance replied, grinning to himself.

Waldo turned to the side, flexing his arm straight down and grabbing his wrist with his other hand to admire his triceps. Then he shielded his eyes, so he could see past his reflection, and looked out the window. "I wonder what all the kids are up to today."

§

RCMP Staff Sergeant Richard Romanowski turned his cruiser onto Main Street as he gave his newest member, Constable Jared Link, a tour of the town. "It may not look like much, but it's a great place to settle in and learn the job. The people are friendly, and nothing too bad ever happens around—"

"Sergeant, look out!"

Romanowski slammed on his brakes just in time to

avoid hitting Joey, who had run out into the street. Joey held up his hands as if he were under arrest. "I'm so sorry, Sergeant Romanowski, but I have to run. Someone's trying to kill me!"

Before either officer could reply, Joey took off down an alley. Just then, another kid appeared. The moment he saw the police car, he froze and then ducked back around the corner.

"Was that a gun in his hand?" Constable Link asked.

"So much for nothing ever happening around here," Romanowski replied. "Hold on!" He turned on his lights and siren and hit the gas.

§

At Matt and Chad's house, the bathroom door opened a crack, and Matt peeked out, his eyeball rotating wildly in its socket as he scanned the hallway for potential assassins.

"Boo!" Chad yelled. The door slammed shut, followed by the sound of Matt hastily locking it.

Chad doubled over with laughter. "That was awesome. Come on, Matt. Are you going to stay in there all day or what?"

"If I have to!" Matt replied, his voice sounding muffled through the door.

"You're not my target. Honest!"

"That's exactly what an assassin would say!"

Chad paused for a moment. He couldn't disagree with that. Then his face lit up. "Tell you what, I'm going to set my water pistol on the floor and then back away to the other end of the hallway. Peek under the door. You'll be able to see it."

Chad did as he promised. He heard some shuffling and saw Matt's shadow as he bent down to look. Then

Matt unlocked the door and peeked out again. "Show me your hands."

Chad raised his hands, revealing he wasn't holding a weapon. When Matt was satisfied, he opened the door all the way and stepped into the hall.

"Finally!" Chad said. "All I wanted was my toothb—" His words were cut off as Matt drew his water pistol and shot Chad three times in the chest, completing soaking his paper target. He pulled the trigger a fourth time for good measure, shooting his brother in the face.

"Gotcha!"

Chad spluttered as he wiped the water from his face. "What? You can't—"

Matt grinned as he held up his victim's information sheet. "Oh yes I can!"

"Give me that!" Chad snatched the paper out of Matt's hand and looked at it. It featured a Polaroid photo of Chad's smiling face. "I can't believe Joyce did this!"

"Did what?" Mrs. Taylor asked, emerging from her bedroom with one hand clutching her bathrobe to hold it shut. Her hair was mussed, her face lined from sleep. "And can you boys keep it down? Some people are trying to sleep around here, you know."

Matt hid his water pistol behind his back as he kicked Chad's gun into the bathroom. "Nothing. We were just—"

Mrs. Taylor leaned forward and squinted, her eyes still not quite adjusted to the daylight. "And why do you have a piece of paper from a coloring book pinned to your pajamas?"

Matt looked down at his target. Chad seized the moment to rip his off and hide it behind his back, along with the information sheet. "This?" Matt said, his mind racing. "Oh, you know, it's something all the kids are doing now. A new trend that started when we were at the coast."

Mrs. Taylor wasn't buying it. "It's a picture of Winnie-the-Pooh. You hate Winnie-the-Pooh."

Matt glanced down at his chest and shrugged. "Yeah, well, all the good pages were taken."

Joyce's bedroom door opened, and she stepped into the hallway in her nightgown, her hair tousled and her eyes nothing but narrow slits.

"I'm still waiting to hear what she has to do with this," Mrs. Taylor said.

"With what?" Joyce inquired.

"This." Chad held up his soaking wet target and scowled at her.

Joyce frowned as she stared at it, and then her eyes opened wide in understanding. "Oh, that." She shrugged. "Completely random assignments. Sorry about your luck." Without another word, she disappeared into the bathroom and closed the door.

"Wait! I need to get my—brilliant," Chad said, crumpling his target and tossing it at Matt. "Out of the game before it even begins." He stalked off toward the kitchen.

Matt smoothed out Chad's target and grinned as he stared at it. "Wait'll the guys hear about this!"

"Would someone please tell me what's going on?" Mrs. Taylor asked.

Matt looked at his mother in surprise, having nearly forgotten she was standing there. "Oh, uh, you know." He held up Chad's target. "Chad's never liked Winnie-the-Pooh either."

As Matt disappeared inside his bedroom, Mrs. Taylor shook her head. "Kids these days. Just when you think you're starting to understand them . . .."

§

49

Constable Link held onto his door handle as Staff Sergeant Romanowski squealed the cruiser around the corner. "Figures this'd happen on your first day," the senior officer growled.

"There he is!" Link said, pointing toward the park.

Romanowski slammed on his brakes. "Go get 'im!"

Constable Link opened his door and jumped out. "Freeze!"

The boy stopped and raised his hands.

"Face down on the ground!"

Once the boy complied, Constable Link approached cautiously, his hand on his weapon, though he didn't draw it. Romanowski was right behind him. When they reached the kid, Constable Link grabbed the boy's hands and put them behind his back, then pulled out his handcuffs.

"You have the right to remain silent. If you do say anything, what you say—"

"Hold on a second," Romanowski said. "Aren't you Bill Gustafson's kid?"

"Yes," the boy replied, glancing up. "I'm Billy. Why are you arresting me?"

"—can be used against you—"

"I said hold on a second, Constable Link. Billy, Joey said you were trying to kill him. Is that true?"

"No! I mean yes. I mean no!"

Romanowski took a deep breath and huffed through his mustache. "You better start talking clearly, son."

"I think I may have solved the mystery, Staff Sergeant." Constable Link held something up for him to see.

"A water pistol, eh?" Romanowski took it from Link and examined it.

"Yes, sir," Billy replied. "It's just a game. I'm not really trying to kill anybody."

"Well, you're going to get somebody killed chasing them into the street like that." He nodded for Link to let him go. The constable put away his handcuffs and then helped Billy to his feet. Romanowski held out the water pistol. "I don't mind you kids having some good clean fun, but keep it off the streets, okay?"

"Yes, sir," Billy replied, his head bowed as he took his gun from Romanowski's outstretched hand.

"And aren't you a little too old for the Smurfs?"

Billy looked up in confusion. "Excuse me?"

"That piece of paper. On your shirt."

Billy looked down at his target. It featured a picture of Papa Smurf, only it was smudged, blue and red paint running down the image. "Oh no! That grass, it must have been wet!" He looked like he was going to cry.

"It's okay, son," Romanowski said. "I'm sure you can get another one."

Billy shook his head, on the verge of tears. "No, I can't." He ripped it off his chest. "Can I go now?"

"Yes, but like I said, be more careful next time, okay?"

"Yes, sir," Billy said. "I'm sorry."

He turned and shuffled off across the park, his head hanging. The two officers watched him in wonder. "A kid his age crying over a page from a coloring book?" Link asked. "Haven't seen that before."

Romanowski shrugged. "Welcome to Milligan Creek. As I was saying, nothing too bad ever happens around here. As for strange, well, that's a completely different story. Have I told you about that radio show yet?"

8

A CLOSE CALL

Mrs. Muller was peeking out the window in the front door of their house when her husband, Dennis, came down the stairs and sat on the bench by the hall closet. "I'm heading out to the Loewens' farm this morning to wire some lights in Fred's new pole shed," he said as he pulled his work boots out from beneath the bench. "Probably be back by lunch, but I'll give you a call if I'm going to be late."

"Mmm-hmm," Mrs. Muller replied.

"What's on your agenda for the day?" Dennis asked as he laced up his boots. When she didn't reply, he glanced up and realized she was still staring out the window. He sat up straight. "Expecting someone?" Still no answer. "Hello, earth to Audrey. Anyone home?" He thumped on the bench, causing her to jump.

"Huh? Oh, uh, no, I'm not—"

"And what the heck is that?"

Mrs. Muller turned to look at him. "What's what?"

"That." He pointed to the target pinned to her chest.

Mrs. Muller looked down at it uncertainly. Then she struck a pose, her hands on her hips as she flashed him a smile. "Do you like it? All the cool kids are wearing them."

Dennis regarded her skeptically. "But you're not a kid. And besides, since when did you become a fan of Mickey Mouse? I thought you were morally opposed to Disney on account of your feminist views."

Before she could answer, they heard footsteps at the top of the stairs, and they both looked up. As soon as Dean saw his parents, he froze.

"Good morning, Dean," Mrs. Muller sang sweetly. "Sleep well?"

"Not really," Dean replied, his hand gripping the bannister in case he had to flee to safety. "I kept dreaming someone was rattling the doorknob to my bedroom."

Mrs. Muller smiled slyly. "Maybe it wasn't a dream."

Dean's eyebrows shot up, and his entire body tensed, ready to bolt.

"Don't tell me you're into this silly trend too," Dennis said.

Dean gave his father a blank look. "Trend? What are you—"

"Don't play dumb," Mrs. Muller said. "The coloring book page. I was just telling your father about it."

"And I was just telling your mother how ridiculous it is. Kids wearing them is one thing, but don't you find it a little embarrassing to have your mother walking around like this?"

"Yes!" Dean replied. "I tried to talk her out of it, but she insisted." He gave his mother a meaningful look.

"See?" Dennis turned back to his wife. "I really think you should reconsider."

"Yes, well, I think you should both mind your own business—that is, if you want to live to see another sunrise." She glared at Dean to emphasize the point. Then, with a final look out the window, she smiled and grabbed her purse. "Ta-ta!"

Mr. Muller watched her go out and then turned back to Dean, his face a mask of confusion. "Did she just threaten us?"

Dean came downstairs and looked out the window as his mother got into her car. "It's nothing you need to worry about, Dad." He clutched his water pistol beneath his jacket. "This is between Mom . . . and me."

After his mother pulled out of the driveway, Dean opened the door a crack and peeked out.

"What are you doing?"

Dean nearly jumped out of this skin at the sound of his father's voice. "What am I what?"

"First your mother and now you. You're acting as if you're scared to go outside."

Dean cleared his throat and straightened his shoulders. "Me? Scared to go outside?" He faked a laugh. "Whatever gave you that idea?" Then his smile faded, and he swallowed hard.

His father folded his arms and eyeballed his son. "So, are you going to go out or what?"

"Uh, maybe later," Dean said, closing the door and racing back upstairs.

Dennis stared after him for a moment and then shook his head as he resumed tying his boots. "Why do I get the feeling I'm the only sane person around here?"

§

Andrew revved the open-cab tractor on his family's farm as he speared a round bale with the silver prongs on the front-end loader and prepared to drive it across the feedlot to use as bedding for the twenty-five head of cattle his father kept. Each year, Mr. Loewen said he was going to get rid of them, but even though the cattle were a lot of work, they were still profitable, and everyone in the family liked having animals around, especially during calving season. Andrew smiled as he watched the new batch of calves, which were already several weeks old, prance and kick in the fresh golden straw as he unrolled the bale. They were always so playful at this age.

As he turned back to get another bale, his eye was drawn to the nearby highway as a semi roared past, honking its horn. Andrew was just in time to see a girl wave to the semi and then turn down their driveway on a pink bicycle, handlebar streamers flying in the wind as if she was ten years old, even though it was clear from her size that the rider was older than that. Andrew parked the tractor and headed toward the house. He still had more work to do with the cattle, and he was anxious to get finished and go into town, so he could hunt down his first victim, but he was curious to find out who the visitor was. Besides, it was time for a mid-morning snack.

As he walked, the breeze caused his target to flutter in the wind. He put his hand on it to ensure it didn't blow away into a puddle or something. That was all he needed, to be taken out of the game before he'd even had a chance to go after his first victim.

As soon as Andrew opened the front door to his house, he heard a female voice that sounded strangely familiar. Suddenly, he realized exactly who it was: Fiona! But why was she at his farm? Then his eyes dropped to the target on his chest. Of course!

Hoping no one had heard him, he quietly backed through the door and had almost managed to shut it when—

"Andrew? Is that you?" It was his mother. Andrew's heart sank. There was no getting away now, especially once he heard the familiar creak of the kitchen floor as she approached the front entrance. She appeared at the top of the three stairs that led up to their kitchen and gave him a funny look as he stood there, half in and half out the door. "What are you doing?"

"Uh, I was thirsty, so I came in to—"

"That's perfect!" Mrs. Loewen exclaimed. "I was just going to call you in. You have a visitor."

"Uh, I do?"

"Yes!" Mrs. Loewen leaned in close. "And it's a girl!" she whispered.

Andrew glanced at the pink bicycle, which was parked conspicuously outside the house. "You don't say."

Mrs. Loewen motioned rapidly with her hand. "Don't just stand there, come in, come in."

"But Mom, the cattle need—"

"The cattle can wait," she said, pulling Andrew inside. "It's rude to keep your company waiting."

With a sigh, Andrew followed her up the stairs.

Just before he entered the kitchen, he paused, wondering if he should just bolt and come up with a story for his mother later, but before he could, she tugged him forward. "Come on!"

When he entered the kitchen, he saw Fiona sitting at the dining table, her back to the wall and her sunglasses on, a big smile on her face. Her Walkman headphones hung around her neck.

"Fiona was just telling me about her eye problems," Mrs. Loewen said.

Andrew gave his mother a skeptical look. "Eye problems? What eye problems?"

"You know," Mrs. Loewen said, pointing to her own eyes. "Hence the sunglasses."

"Oh yeah, right."

"Well, don't just stand there like a post, sit down, sit down," Mrs. Loewen said, pulling out a chair. Andrew had no choice but to take it. He sat down and tried to look anywhere but at Fiona, who sat across the table from him, grinning.

"So, Andrew, this is your farm, hey?"

Andrew nodded, still not looking at her. "Yup."

"Nice place. But it was quite the grueling bike ride to get here."

"I'll bet."

"I borrowed my neighbor's bike. It doesn't have any gears. Hard to peddle against the wind. But I'm sure you know all about that, having lived out here your entire life."

Andrew nodded, pursing his lips.

"Andrew, come on now, don't be rude. Talk to our visitor," Mrs. Loewen scolded as she set two glasses of lemonade on the table along with a plate of cookies. "They're thimble cookies," she added, smiling at Fiona. "I made them myself with my own homemade raspberry jam, grown right here in our garden. Help yourself. And don't mind Andrew," she added in a stage whisper, holding the back of her hand to the side of her mouth. "He's just a bit bashful. Especially around girls."

Andrew scowled at her. "Mom!"

Mrs. Loewen grinned and then pranced out of the kitchen. "I'll be in my sewing room in case you need anything!"

"Thanks, Mrs. Loewen," Fiona said, smiling. "You're too kind." She waited until Mrs. Loewen was gone and then turned back to Andrew. "Your mom's nice."

Andrew sniffed. "A little too nice."

Fiona tossed her hair, unrattled by Andrew's comment. "So, you like living way out here?"

Andrew shrugged.

"Do you ever get lonely?"

He crossed his arms. "Not really."

"It must feel pretty vulnerable though," Fiona said,

leaning forward and resting her chin on her fist. "All alone . . . out here. No one to protect you . . . in case something goes wrong."

Andrew frowned at her. "What do you mean? What could possibly go—"

All at once, he realized that while she was leaning on her left hand, her right hand was out of sight under the table. He froze, his hands gripping the edge of the table as he glared at Fiona. "You wouldn't dare."

She grinned. "Maybe I already have."

He looked down at his target, his eyes flaring. "What? How could you—"

His target was still dry, but when his eyes returned to Fiona, her water gun was pointed right at him.

"Goodbye, Andrew."

Just as she pulled the trigger, he ducked, and her shot splattered on the wall behind him. Not wasting a second, he somersaulted across the kitchen floor, shots from Fiona's water gun exploding all around him. Then he made a mad dash for the front door.

Outside, he looked around frantically for somewhere to hide. Then he heard the door open behind him. With no time to lose, he jumped onto the only means of escape available—Fiona's pink bike—and pedaled like a madman toward the highway, handlebar streamers flying in the wind behind him.

Fiona smiled as she watched him go. She tucked her gun into the waistband of her shorts as Mrs. Loewen burst out the front door.

"What the dickens is going on?" Mrs. Loewen exclaimed. Then she spotted her son, pedaling down the driveway as if his life depended on it. "Andrew? Andrew Loewen, get back here with Fiona's bike!" She watched in shock as Andrew ignored her command and turned onto the highway toward town, standing up so he could pedal harder to gain speed. She turned back to Fiona. "I'm terribly sorry, dear. Honestly, I don't know what has gotten into that boy. I knew he was bashful, but I had no idea he was a thief! Let's jump in the car, and we can—"

"I'm the one who should apologize, Mrs. Loewen," Fiona replied. "I think I must have said something that upset him."

"Well, nothing you could have said merits being treated like this. Just wait until I get my hands on him. Come on. After we get your bike, I'll give you a ride back to town."

"I don't want to impose, Mrs. Loewen."

"Don't be ridiculous. It's the least I can do."

She started for the garage and then looked back when she heard a truck turn into the driveway. "Now what?" Only then did she realize it was Mr. Muller, who had come to do some electrical work on the pole shed. Mrs. Loewen and Fiona waited until he pulled up. When he rolled down the window of his flatbed work truck, his face was red with laughter.

"Has the entire world gone nuts or is it just me?"

"I take it you saw Andrew?" Mrs. Loewen asked.

"Saw him? I almost hit the ditch I was laughing so hard. Did he lose a bet or something?"

"No, but he's going to lose a whole lot more than that when I get my hands on him. Now if you'll excuse us, Dennis, I need to run this young lady back into town, seeing as her source of transportation has just been abducted. Why don't you go inside and grab some lemonade and thimble cookies before you get started? We were just about to have a snack before Andrew lost his mind."

"Sounds good to me," Dennis said, his truck's engine rumbling to a halt as he turned it off.

Mrs. Loewen put her arm around Fiona. "As for you,

young lady, at least we can enjoy a bit of girl time on the way in to town. I get starved for female company out here sometimes with no one but Andrew and my husband to talk to. For starters, who does your hair? It's beautiful!"

Fiona grinned and flicked her curly locks over one shoulder as Andrew's mom led her toward the garage. "Mrs. Loewen, you really are too kind."

9

THIS GAME SUCKS!

The electric motor for the overhead door on the Mullers' garage growled to life. Shafts of morning sunlight pierced the building's dust-filled interior as the door began to rise. The sunbeams revealed Joyce, who was busily arranging numerous items on a wooden fold-out table. She looked up from her work when she heard a commotion outside and was surprised to see a number of kids waiting for her. She smiled and approached the group.

"Wow, I didn't expect so many customers already! You must have been a busy little bunch of assassins overnight. Come on over to the table, and turn in your bounties."

She sat behind the table as the kids formed a line in front of it, their victims' water-smeared targets in hand as they eyed the various items laid out before them. The items included umbrellas, water balloons, plastic buckets, water balloon launchers made from surgical tubing and funnels, garden hoses, an inflatable kiddie pool, water sprinklers, and various types of high-powered water guns.

Billy was the first kid in line. Joyce's face melted in concern when she looked at his eyes, which were still red from crying. "Billy, what's the matter?"

"I took myself out trying to kill Joey," he said, holding

up his smeared target. "And I almost got arrested in the process. It was an accident—the police made me lie on my stomach on some wet grass. Is there any way you can let me stay in?"

Joyce grimaced and sucked air through her teeth as she shook her head. "I'm afraid not, Billy. A rule's a rule. But don't worry. I'm sure someone will want to bring you back into the game soon. Maybe even the person who was supposed to take you out. Now if you'll just give me your target and the information package for your victim, I'll inform the person who was supposed to assassinate you—"

"Whoo-hoo!"

Joyce and the others looked up in surprise as Matt skidded to a stop on his bike, sending up a cloud of dust from Dean's gravel driveway. He hopped off his bike and threw it to the ground, holding Chad's target up for all to see. "Matt Taylor one, Chad Taylor zero!" He slapped the target on the table in front of Joyce.

"Uh, there's a line here, Matt, in case you didn't notice," Joyce said.

"Is there?" Matt looked around in surprise at the other kids as they coughed and waved away the dust. "Sorry about that." He picked up his target and went to the back of the line.

Just then, Andrew zoomed up on Fiona's pink bike, streamers flying, and nailed the brakes, sending up another cloud of dust. He tossed the bike to the side and somersaulted into the garage, drawing his water pistol in one fluid motion as he took up a defensive position just inside the door, his eyes peeled for any potential attackers.

"Nice wheels, Andrew," Matt said, snickering, "but you're just supposed to kill your victim, not steal their ride."

"The bike doesn't belong to my victim," Andrew replied, his eyes scanning the row of lilac bushes that ran along the sidewalk in front of Dean's house. "It belongs to my would-be assassin."

"And who might that be?"

Before Andrew could reply, Mrs. Loewen pulled into the driveway, Fiona in the passenger seat. Andrew's face went pale. "Uh-oh." He ducked behind a tool cupboard before his mother could see him.

"Quick!" Matt cried. "Hide your guns!"

Joyce pulled a sheet over the table as the other kids tucked their guns out of sight.

Fiona opened the car door and got out. "Thanks for the ride, Mrs. Loewen—and the girl talk. We should do it again sometime. As you can see, my bike is exactly where I thought it would be."

"Yes, but where's Andrew?" Mrs. Loewen leaned over the passenger seat and looked out the open window. "Matt, have you seen him?"

Matt looked around and then turned back to Mrs. Loewen and shrugged. "He was here a minute ago."

"Well, if you see him again, tell him I'm looking for him. He's got a lot of explaining to do."

Matt nodded. "I will, Mrs. Loewen."

She put the car in "drive" and was about to pull away when she paused. "What are you kids up to here anyway? And where's Dean?"

"I'm right here, Mrs. Loewen," Dean said, emerging from the back of the garage, which he had just entered through the side door. "We're just, you know, hanging out."

"You'd think on a day like today, you'd all want to be down by the pool."

Dean shrugged. "That gets a little boring after a while." He winced slightly and touched his back. "Not to mention painful."

Mrs. Loewen nodded. "I guess so. Anyway, if you do

see Andrew . . .."

"We'll be sure to let him know you're looking for him," Matt replied.

As soon as she drove off, Andrew stepped out of the shadows, his water pistol pointing at Fiona. "This is neutral turf. You're not allowed to kill anybody in here."

"And *you're* not allowed to kill your assassin," Fiona said, stepping closer to the garage, which caused Andrew to back up instinctively. "Not that I'm out to kill you."

Andrew frowned. "What are you talking about? You just tried to—"

Before he could finish, Fiona reached out and casually shot Debbie, the girl who was standing in line in front of Matt, right in the chest.

"What?" Debbie cried. "But I'm on neutral—"

"Technically, you're not inside the garage," Joyce said, pointing at Debbie's feet, which were on the gravel just outside the overhead door. "Which means you're fair game." In response, Debbie hopped into the garage, as did the other kids in line, but Joyce shook her head. "Too late."

Fiona held out her hand to Debbie and smiled, her eyes still on Andrew. "Your target, please."

Debbie huffed and then ripped off her target and slapped it into Fiona's hand. "Fine, but this hardly seems fair."

"And your victim's information," Fiona continued.

Debbie growled. "This is such a stupid game!" She pulled out a piece of paper and shoved it into Fiona's hand.

Andrew stared at Fiona in confusion. "But if I wasn't your victim, then why did you—"

"Just to let you know I can—and I will—when the time comes." She grinned at Andrew, who caught a glimpse of his worried face in the reflection of her sunglasses before she turned to look at all the other kids assembled there, ending on Matt. "To let *all* of you know."

Matt crossed his arms in defiance. "Hmph."

"But you shot at me!" Andrew protested. "And now my mother thinks . . . but that isn't—"

"Moo."

Andrew and the others turned to look as Ben approached, towing the life-sized cow he had built in wood shop a couple of months earlier.

"How's it going, Ben?" Matt asked. "That cow your first victim?"

"No, but I was hoping someone here could help me fix it."

"What's the matter with it?"

"It won't give any milk."

Matt glanced at the others, a smile burgeoning on his face. "Uh, you do know the cow's not real, right?"

"Yeah, but I rigged it up so that something would still come out if you squeezed its udder."

"Well, I don't know anything about mechanical cows," Matt said, jabbing his thumb back toward the garage, "but I'm sure Andrew can help you. At least his family owns some real ones."

Andrew tucked his water pistol into the waistband of his pants as he edged across the garage, his eyes still on Fiona. "I suppose I can take a look at it."

When he reached the door, he took a quick look around to ensure no would-be assassins were lurking outside and then approached Ben and his cow. "What did you say was the matter—"

Before he could finish, a jet of water shot out of the cow's mouth and struck Andrew in the face. "What the—" His words were cut off as another blast hit him in the chest. He wiped the water out of his eyes and shook his head vigorously. Suddenly, his eyes shot open. "Oh no! My target!" Sure enough, when he looked down, it was dripping wet, a rainbow of colors running onto his shirt. When he looked up, Ben was laughing silently, one hand clutching his chest as he held out the other toward Andrew. "Your target, please."

Andrew glared at him for a moment and then ripped his target off his chest and threw it at Ben. "Debbie's right," he said, stomping away. "This game sucks."

As Andrew walked away, Chad rode up from the opposite direction on his bike. He paused and watched Andrew's retreating form before turning back to the group. "What'd I miss?"

"Nothing," Fiona said, stepping forward. "In fact, you're just in time."

"For what?" Chad asked.

Fiona smiled. "To join my team."

10

POWER UP!

"What?" Chad stared at Fiona, stunned.

"It's in the rules," Joyce said. "Players can power up by getting a new weapon, something to defend themselves, or bringing a 'dead' player back into the game."

"I realize that," Chad said. "I helped create the rules. But really? Me? Why me?"

Fiona grinned. "I'll have all of you on my team . . . eventually." She directed this last word toward Matt.

In response, Matt stepped out of line and slapped his bounty on the table. "Fat chance. Give me a new gun. The biggest one you've got."

Joyce slid a battery-powered Super Soaker toward him. "Think you can handle it, pardner?" she asked in a Western accent. It was a huge gun, complete with a reserve tank that served as the gun's butt stock. Matt picked up the gun, tested the weight of it in his hand, and then sighted down the barrel, pretending to take a shot. "Not bad."

Fiona snickered. "Better do some target practice. You're going to need it."

As if to emphasize her point, she held out her water pistol and shot another kid, Darrel, who had just jogged up to the garage. He looked down at his soaked target, his victim's bounty clutched in his hand. "What the . . .?"

"I'll take Andrew," Fiona said, ripping Darrel's target off his chest and slapping it on the table.

"What?" Darrel sputtered. "But you can't—"

"Oh yes she can," Joyce said. "Technically speaking, Fiona was outside the garage, and so were you, Darrel."

"But that's puppy guarding!" Matt protested.

Joyce shrugged. "Maybe so, but we didn't make a rule against it."

"Yeah, but still." Matt frowned, thought for a moment, and then set the Super Soaker back on the table. "On second thought," Matt began, Billy rising to his feet in the hope Matt would choose him for his team, "I'm going to be a purist on this one. No extra weapons, no defensive items, and no additional team members." Billy sank back into his seat in disappointment.

"Are you sure about that?" Joyce asked. She nodded at the growing line of assassins, who had already taken out their victims. "It's an assassin-shoot-assassin world out there."

Matt glared at Fiona. "*Some* people may need an army to win this game, but not me." Fiona held Matt's gaze and grinned, infuriating him further. "My water pistol, please." Matt said, holding his hand out to his sister, his eyes still on Fiona. Joyce slapped the gun into his palm. "May the best *man* win." Matt cast a sidelong glance at Chad. Then, after taking a brief look around to make sure the coast was clear, he ran out the door, grabbed his bike, and pedaled away.

"Even *I* want to take him out after that," Chad said. He turned to Fiona and held out his hand. "Partners?"

She smiled and shook it. "Until the end."

"Let's go find Andrew," Chad said, slipping on a pair of black sunglasses that matched Fiona's and grabbing another pair for Andrew. "I can't wait to tell him we're a team!" He paused. "That is, if it's okay with you, Fiona."

She smiled. "I wouldn't have it any other way."

After Chad and Fiona left, Joyce went through the process of confirming kills and handing out rewards to the other players. Some, like Fiona, chose to bring another player back into the game to join their team. Others picked an item from the table to boost their defensive or offensive capabilities.

"What's this?" a girl named Bonnie asked, holding up a strange-looking electronic device.

"A sprinkler timer," Joyce replied.

"What's it for?"

"Think about it," Joyce said. "You can set it to turn on someone's sprinkler at any time of day . . . or night."

Bonnie pondered it for a moment, and then a wicked smile crept across her face. "I think I know just what to do with it."

When she left, another boy, Ian, stepped up to the table. He scanned the various items available and then turned to Joyce. "What if we don't see anything we want?"

"Do you have another option in mind?"

"Actually . . .." He leaned forward and whispered into Joyce's ear.

When he was finished, Joyce sat back and nodded. "Sounds good to me."

And so it continued for much of the morning, until the only player left in the garage was Billy.

"See?" he said, throwing his hands up in defeat. "I knew no one would pick me to be on their team."

"Not so fast," Mrs. Muller said, stepping into the garage and slapping her first victim's target on the table. "From now on, you're working for me."

Billy swallowed hard. "I am?"

71

"Yes."

He looked Mrs. Muller up and down, sighed, and then turned back to Joyce. "Uh, can I have my water pistol back, please?"

Joyce was about to hand it to him, but Mrs. Muller snatched it from her hand. "Not so fast."

"But Mrs. Muller," Billy protested, "if I'm going to help you kill somebody, I need a gun."

"Not yet you don't." She handed him a pair of pink neon sunglasses as she donned her own. "Not until you've completed your training."

Billy looked at the sunglasses in despair. "Training?"

Mrs. Muller approached him menacingly. "You're weak, Billy. You hear me? Weak. But by the time I get through with you, you'll be a lean, mean, killing machine. Now let's go."

Billy tried to swallow again, but it sounded more like a gulp. "I don't know, Mrs. Muller, maybe I'd should ask my mom—"

"Your mother?" Mrs. Muller got in his face and stared him down like a drill sergeant. "The game's hardly started, and you're already asking for your mother? Don't you know telling adults about this game is against the rules?"

"Yeah, but—"

"While you two sort things out, I'm heading home," Joyce said, standing up. "I'll put a sign on the door saying I'll be back this afternoon to collect more bounties." She paused for a moment and scribbled the note on a piece of paper. "Funny, I saw Dean around here a few minutes ago, but he suddenly disappeared. I wonder how he's doing."

Mrs. Muller stood in the doorway and scanned her surroundings. "Oh, he's out there . . . somewhere. But if I know Dean, it won't be long until he's crawling in here with his target soaked and his tail tucked between his legs. Now come on, Billy. Time to put on your big boy pants. It may be too late for my son, but there's still plenty of time to make a man out of you."

"Yes, Mrs. Muller." Billy gave Joyce a mournful look as Mrs. Muller dragged him outside.

Joyce chuckled and shook her head as she walked over and hit the button to close the overhead door. "Poor Billy."

As the overhead garage door eased down, Dean lay flat on his stomach under the lilac bushes a few yards away, watched his mother drag Billy down the street, the sullen boy still protesting.

"Come back with my tail between my legs, hey?" Dean said, looking down at a photo of his victim. "We'll see about that." He slithered out from beneath the lilacs and crept down the street, heading in the opposite direction of his mother and Billy.

A block away, a shadow detached itself from a building and followed Dean, water pistol in hand.

11

THE MYSTERY BOX

Moo-moo . . . Moo-moo . . . .

"I'll get it!"

Ben's six-year-old sister, Emily, raced to the front door, alerted to the fact that they had a visitor by the family's custom-made doorbell, which bellowed like a hungry cow demanding its supper. It was a gift to Ben that his father had installed to help soften his son's disappointment over their recent move into town.

When she opened the door, on the front step was an enormous cardboard box, the kind in which a dishwasher or an oven might be delivered, only this box was wrapped in colorful cow-themed wrapping paper, including black-and-white ribbon and an enormous bow. She eyed it curiously and then looked around for the person who had delivered it, but no one was in sight.

"Who is it, honey?" her mother called from inside the house.

"I don't know, but I hope it's for me!"

Standing on her tiptoes, she peeked on top of the box and saw a tag attached to the ribbon. The moment she read it, her face fell. "Aww . . . it's for Ben!"

"What's for Ben?" her mother, Mrs. Somerville, asked,

walking up behind her and wiping her hands on a dish-towel. "Omigosh!" she cried when she saw the box. She threw her towel over her shoulder and read the gift tag. As she did, Emily glared at her, hands on her hips.

"What's so special about Ben that he gets a great big present and I don't?"

"I don't know, Emily. I don't even know who it's—"

"Moo."

They both looked back into the house as Ben approached. Mrs. Somerville smiled. "Ben, look at this! Do you know anyone who would send you such a huge present? Your birthday's not for another three months."

Ben's face lit up when he saw the wrapping paper, but then his eyes narrowed in suspicion, his hand moving instinctively to the target on his chest. "Who delivered it?"

His mother looked at Emily in anticipation of a response, but the little girl just held up her hands in bewilderment. "I don't know. It was here when I opened the door."

Ben crossed his arms and stared at the box.

"Well, aren't you going to open it?" his mother asked.

"Yeah, Ben, open it!" Emily said. "Who knows? It's big enough there could be a baby cow inside, just like you've always wanted. Look, it even has cows on the wrapping paper." She knocked on the box with her knuckles. "Hello in there, baby cow, anybody home?"

Mrs. Somerville smiled warmly at her son. "Or maybe it's a gift from a secret admirer. Maybe it's from that new girl who moved to town. What's her last name again, Prickleberrybush?"

Ben scowled at his mother. "Pickleberrybush." He stepped forward, examined the box for a moment, and then stepped back and shook his head, the cowlicks on the back of his head bouncing with the movement. "I don't want it."

"What?" She looked at him in shock. "Why not?"

Ben shook his head slowly. "I don't know, but it just doesn't feel right."

"But Ben—"

"Moo."

Before his mother could press him any further, he retreated into the house. She and Emily watched him go and then turned back to the box.

"If Ben doesn't want it, can I have it?" Emily asked, craning her head to look at her mother.

"No, it's addressed to Ben."

"But he doesn't want it."

"It doesn't matter."

"That's stupid. What are we going to do with it?"

Mrs. Somerville sighed. "I guess I'll have your father put it in the garage until I can talk some sense into your brother." She turned and headed back into the house. "Alex . . . ."

Emily scowled at her mother and then glared at the box. "Stupid present." She was about to slam the door on it when—

"Achoo!"

Emily froze, her hand still on the doorknob. "Who did that?"

§

Mr. Muller was sitting at the kitchen table slurping canned mushroom soup from a spoon when he heard the front door open. He looked toward the door as he reached for a package of soda crackers.

"Dean? Is that you?"

He was about to crumble a handful of crackers into his bowl when his wife entered the kitchen sporting her neon-pink sunglasses. He smirked. "Hi, Audrey. What's with the—" He paused when Billy shuffled in forlornly behind her, pushing up his own pair of pink sunglasses, which kept slipping down his nose.

"Can we have lunch first, Mrs. Muller?" Billy asked, eyeing the mushroom soup hungrily. "Please?"

"Definitely not," Mrs. Muller said, plunking her purse onto the table. "Not until you've completed your first round of training."

"Training?" Billy wailed. "But Mrs. Muller—"

"Head out to the backyard," she said, holding the rear screen door open for him. "I'll be out in a minute. And no trying to escape, or I'll tie to you a lamp post on Main Street and auction you off to the highest bidder!"

"Yes, Mrs. Muller." Billy hung his head and trudged out the door, realizing protest was futile.

Mrs. Muller let the screen door slam shut and then walked over to the refrigerator. Only then did she notice her husband staring at her in confusion, his hand full of crushed crackers that he had yet to drop into his soup bowl. She furrowed her brow. "What are you looking at?"

"Nice glasses."

"Hmph." She opened the fridge and began rooting around inside.

"Care to explain, Audrey?"

"I would . . ." She stuck her head out of the fridge and looked at him. ". . . but then I'd have to kill you." She smiled sarcastically and then grabbed two juice boxes and a couple of nectarines and went out the back door.

"Get off that trampoline, Billy!" she yelled as she descended the back steps. "What do you think this is, pre-school?"

Mr. Muller thought about going out and trying to rescue Billy, but if he did, who would rescue him? With a shrug, he dropped his crackers into his soup and continued eating.

§

Emily swung the door wide open and scanned the front yard, but no one was there. She was about to peek behind the box to see if someone was hiding back there when—

"Achoo!"

She jumped back in shock. So, she hadn't been imagining things after all. "I knew it! There is a baby cow inside." She grabbed the box with both hands and shook it. "Hello, little baby cow. Moo for me!"

"Hey, quit it!" a boy's voice said. "You're going to tip me over!"

Emily stopped rocking the box and stared at it in wonder. "A talking cow? Wait till Ben hears about this. Hey, Mom!"

"Wait!" the boy said. "It's not a baby cow—which is called a calf, by the way. It's Ian. I'm just trying to play a trick on—"

"What is it, Emily?" Mrs. Somerville asked, stepping onto the front porch.

Emily looked from her mother to the box and then back again, unsure how to respond. "Oh, uh, nothing. I was just going to tell you that . . . I'll be playing in the front yard. In case you need me to do any chores or anything."

Mrs. Somerville put her hands on her hips and gave Emily a funny look. "Chores? Since when do *you* do any chores around—on second thought . . .."

"Bye, Mom!" Emily ran off toward the swing set before her mother could give her an assignment.

Once her mother went inside, Emily crept back toward the box and rapped on it with her knuckles. "Hey, Ian, you still in there?"

"Where else would I be?"

"Why are you trying to play a trick on Ben?"

"It's part of a game."

"What kind of game?"

"I can't say."

"Can I play?"

"No, but you can help me."

Emily crossed her arms and glared at the box. "Why should I help you? You won't even let me play your stupid game."

"Sorry, what I meant to say was, helping me is part of the game."

Her face brightened somewhat, though she was still skeptical. "Oh yeah? What do you want me to do?"

"Get Ben to come outside."

"Why?"

"So I can surprise him."

Emily cocked her head to one side. "Are you dressed like a cow or something? Is that the surprise?"

"Uh, no."

"Then what's so surprising about him finding you in a box?"

"You'll see."

Just then, the front door opened, and Mr. Somerville came out. His eyes widened when he saw the box. "Wow, your mother wasn't kidding." He bent down and wrapped his arms around it, but it was too heavy to lift. "Geez, I wonder what's inside. Anyway, guess I'll have to get the trolley." He headed toward their detached garage.

Emily waited until he was out of earshot and then turned back to the box. "What'll you give me if I help you?"

"I don't know. What do you want?"

Emily thought for a moment and then smiled. "Candy! Lots and lots of candy."

"Okay, I'll get you some candy. Now get your brother."

"Not just any candy. I want Bottlecaps, Sweetarts, Mike and Ikes, Fun Dip—"

"I'll get you whatever you want! Just go get Ben!"

"Not until you moo for me."

"What?"

Emily crossed her arms and stared at the box. "You heard me."

Ian was quiet for a second. Then . . . "Moo."

"Louder!"

"Moo!"

"Louder!"

"MOO!"

"Emily?"

She looked up as her father approached from the garage pushing a two-wheeled trolley. "What's with all the racket?"

"Oh, just practicing my cow sounds," she said, giggling to herself as she opened the door. "Oh, Ben . . .," she called, letting the screen door close behind her as she went inside.

Mr. Somerville watched her go and then shook his head as he slid the lip of the trolley under one edge of the box. "That's all I need," he said, grunting as he tilted the box back toward himself and onto the trolley. "Another kid obsessed with cows."

12

MISS MILLIGAN CREEK

A row of photographs pinned to a bulletin board greeted the members of the Miss Milligan Creek committee as they drifted into the boardroom at the town hall to determine who would win the coveted title. The victor would receive a cash prize, a plaque, a photo in the newspaper, and a featured position on top of the town's new fire truck in the Milligan Creek Daze parade, which was set to take place the following Saturday. Like previous years, the photos featured Milligan Creek's finest young teenage girls, their smiling faces illuminating the room with the hope of a new and better tomorrow. However, this year's crop of finalists had a decidedly different twist.

"Sunglasses and headphones? On all of them? And what's that pinned to her chest?" Mayor Michael Bondar lifted his eyeglasses and leaned in close to ensure he wasn't seeing things. "A page ripped out of a coloring book? Is this some kind of newfangled fad?"

"Sunglasses or not, I think she's the prettiest," said Kelvin Brown, a heavyset man with a shiny domed head and a fringe of brown hair as he pointed at one of the photos. He was the accountant at the Milligan Creek Co-op. "Or maybe she is. Or even her." He gripped his double chin with his thumb and index finger as he cradled his elbow with his other hand and furrowed his brow, as if struggling to figure out why the Co-op's books wouldn't balance. "Oh, man, it's so hard to decide."

"Not that this is a beauty contest," Abigail Kwasnitza said as she sashayed into the room, flipping her long blond hair dramatically out of her face. "But if it were, *she* would be the winner." She tapped a photo with her perfectly manicured index finger, which was decorated with a bright red fake fingernail. The photo featured a young teenage girl who was the spitting image of Abigail—apart from the sunglasses and headphones.

Kelvin narrowed his eyes at the aging beauty queen as she took a seat at the conference table and pulled out a pocket mirror to check her makeup, which was so thick, it looked like it had been applied with a putty knife. Abigail ran the town's beauty salon and also held a seat on the town council. "I still don't understand how *you* got on this committee," Kelvin said. "Isn't it a conflict of interest, seeing as your daughter is one of the contestants?"

"Abigail only has one vote," Otto Nimigeers reminded the group as he entered. He was the editor of the *Milligan Creek Review*. "And I'm sure she wouldn't use her position on the committee to influence the other members' vote in any way, would you, Abigail?" Otto smiled at her, though it looked more like a grimace. They had a long history together, a sore point being when Abigail won the title of prom queen after Otto's girlfriend, now his wife, was disqualified due to an obscure technicality, though it was rumored Abigail had somehow influenced the decision.

Abigail gave him a sick smile and then snapped her compact mirror shut. "Don't be bitter, Otto. It's not a flattering look on you."

"Well, I'm sure we can all be adults about this," Mayor

Bondar said, taking his seat. "I have every confidence in your ability to make the best choice for the contestants and for our town."

Kelvin paused at his chair and looked at the boardroom table, which was empty except for a glistening jug of ice water, several tall glasses, and a folder in front of each seat, which contained the contestants' application forms. "Hey, wasn't there supposed to be doughnuts at this meeting? You said if I came to this meeting, there would be doughnuts." He cast an accusing glare at Mayor Bondar.

"I'm sorry, Kelvin, I—"

"Oops, that reminds me." Abigail snapped her fingers and leaned back in her chair. "Oh, Thelma . . . .." In response to her call, Abigail's assistant scurried into the room with a pink box of doughnuts from the bakery, fresh and warm and filling the air with a delicious aroma.

"Sorry I'm late, Abigail," Thelma said. "But I wanted to make sure they were fresh out of the deep fryer."

"Especially for you, Kelvin," Abigail said, winking at him. Kelvin gave her a shy smile as the dome of his head reddened slightly. He'd had a crush on her ever since seventh grade, and she never failed to exploit it. "Thanks, Abigail. I'm starving." He licked his lips in anticipation as Thelma handed the box to him. "Thank you, Thelma."

Thelma smiled. "Don't mention it." She turned and left the room, winking in response to Abigail's slight nod.

Otto leaned over and glared at Abigail. "Up to your old tricks, hey?" he whispered.

She offered him a smug smile as she watched Kelvin bite into a chocolate-glazed Long John dusted with rainbow sprinkles. "They're sure good, aren't they, Kelvin?"

"Oh, man, so good." Kelvin sighed in delight as he took another bite. It didn't occur to him that Abigail probably hadn't eaten a doughnut in decades due to her efforts to maintain her slim figure. He held out the box to Otto. "Want one?" he asked, his mouth full of doughnut and a dab of brown frosting and sprinkles on the tip of his nose. "Abigail brought them for me, but I'm happy to share."

Otto offered another pained smile. "No thanks, Kelvin." He turned to the mayor. "Can we get this meeting started? I have a paper to put out tomorrow."

"We're still missing one member of our committee," Mayor Bondar said. He looked at the round, silver-framed wall clock. It had been salvaged from the old elementary school, which had been torn down and replaced with a new one in a different location five years earlier. "I wonder where—"

"Sorry I'm late!" Henrietta Blunt said as she bustled into the room, taking off her Wetlands Unlimited ball cap and plunking herself into one of the black swivel chairs that surrounded the conference table. She was in charge of the Milligan Creek Heritage Marsh, a huge protected wetlands habitat located fifteen minutes north of town. "Had a bit of a crisis down at the marsh today. It was the strangest thing. An American Kestrel was dive-bombing a—"

"I'm sure we're all *dying* to hear your story, Henrietta," Abigail said, her voice oozing sarcasm. "But time is money." She tapped her diamond-studded watch. "I have hair to perm, and those chemicals won't apply themselves."

"Speaking of which," Henrietta said, shuffling through the folder in front of her, "I didn't see a question about the environment on the application form, like I suggested. If we had included one, Julia Onofreychuk would win hands down. I've never seen a more committed volunteer."

"A dedication to the environment is certainly important," Mayor Bondar said, smoothing the long strands of hair that were slicked across his shiny bald pate. "But what we're looking for is a girl with a well-rounded personality, someone who reflects the diversity and ingenuity of our little town. It would be unfair to narrow things down to a single criterion."

"In that case, I vote we make this easier on ourselves and eliminate one of the contestants right out of the gate," Abigail said.

"Eliminate? But why?" Mayor Bondar asked in dismay. "And who?"

"Her." Abigail stood up and ripped one of the photos off the bulletin board, tossing it onto the table.

Everyone leaned in close to read the name at the bottom of the photo. "Fiona Pickleberrybush?" Mayor Bondar looked up at Abigail. "Why would you want to eliminate her?"

"Yes, Abigail, why would you want to eliminate her?" Otto asked, sitting back and crossing his arms. "Scared of a little competition?"

"Of all the applications I read, hers was certainly the one that stood out," Henrietta interjected. She pulled out Fiona's application form and read her credentials to the group. "Honor roll at school for the last three years. Volunteer at the SPCA *and* at the nursing home. School sports reporter for the local newspaper," she added, glancing up. "Maybe you can recruit her for your paper, Otto."

"Maybe I already have." Otto crossed his arms smugly and smiled at Abigail.

Henrietta turned back to the form. "It says here that she even launched her own lawn care business. All before the tender age of fourteen." She snapped the folder shut. "Sounds like the perfect candidate to me—if she had something on her resume about the environment."

"Lawns are part of the environment," Kelvin reminded her as he bit into a doughnut with sparkly green sprinkles on top.

Henrietta thought about it for a second and then nodded. "I can't argue with that, Kelvin."

"Well, she sounds perfectly boring to me," Abigail said. "A regular Goody Two-shoes."

"Don't we *want* Miss Milligan Creek to be a good person?" Otto asked.

"Of course," Abigail replied. "But we still have one big problem."

"What's that?" Mayor Bondar inquired.

"She just moved here."

"So?" Otto replied. "The rules don't mention anything about a minimum residency requirement."

"Well, I vote they should," Abigail said. "Starting now. It's hardly fair that some interloper can come into our town and steal the title from girls who have poured their entire lives into serving this community."

Otto sat back and looked at her. "Serving this community?" He grabbed his folder off the table and rifled through it until he found the application for Abigail's daughter. "What did Natalie say she has spent the summer doing? Trying out different nail polish colors on her dog?"

Ignoring Otto, Abigail raised her hand. "I vote we institute a minimum one-year residency requirement. Anyone second the motion?" She looked around the table until her glare came to rest on Kelvin. He had just bitten into a jam-filled doughnut, his third, completely oblivious to what was going on. But when he saw Abigail's glare, he slowly raised his sugar-coated hand, looking around uncertainly.

Otto sighed. "Really, Abigail? At any rate, you're out of order. Only the chairperson can propose a motion. Mayor Bondar? What do you think?"

All eyes turned to the mayor, who shifted uncomfortably in his seat. He hated conflict, but he could see there was no easy way out of this situation. "I agree that Fiona's new to town," he began after thinking things over for a moment. "And from what I've heard, she's made quite the fuss ever since she arrived. Awarding her the title would be a great way to welcome Fiona and her family to the community. But if we do, it's bound to make the other girls jealous. On the other hand, she's more than qualified, not to mention beautiful. Just picture her up there on the new fire truck during the parade. It'd put a wonderful new face on our town." He smiled as he leaned back in his chair and pictured the image in his mind.

"Maybe we could even convince her to take off the sunglasses and headphones," Kelvin said. "At least for the parade," he added.

"No one asked you, Kelvin," Abigail snapped. He frowned and then buried his face in another doughnut.

"Well, Mr. Mayor?" Otto asked. "What about the residency requirement?"

Mayor Bondar sighed. "With all due respect, Abigail, I hardly think it's fair to introduce a new rule this late in the game. Perhaps it's something we can consider for next year."

Otto smiled in triumph as Abigail clenched her teeth and then sank slowly into her chair.

The mayor clapped his hands together. "Well, now that that's all sorted out, are we ready to put it to a vote?"

"Not so fast," Henrietta said, squinting at Fiona's application. "I appreciate what Kelvin said about lawns being part of the environment, but on second thought, we all know that a bright, green, weed-free lawn is usually an indicator of excessive use of fertilizer and herbicides. How do we know Fiona's prospective reign as Miss Milligan Creek won't lead to the environmental devastation of our town?"

The other committee members rolled their eyes in

frustration. Mayor Bondar sighed and then poured himself a tall glass of water. Something told him this was going to be a *long* afternoon.

13

A GOLDEN OPPORTUNITY

His eyes peeled to ensure no assassins were lurking in the shadows, Dean crept down the back alley east of Main Street, leapfrogging from dumpster to telephone pole to garbage can until he reached the loading dock behind the Milligan Creek Co-op. Sitting in front of the dock was the store's delivery van, ready to make its daily run of grocery orders to seniors and shut-ins around the community. The doors to the loading dock were open, and suddenly, Dean heard voices approaching from inside the store. Worried that one of them might be his assassin, he ducked into the bottle cage and hid behind a palette of pop bottles ready to be recycled.

"I'm sending two of you out today, because we've got a lot of orders to deliver, and some big ones too." Curly-haired Co-op manager Bob Linnen handed the delivery list to Patrick, the older of the two stock boys he was sending out on the road, Darcy being the younger one. "But no fooling around, and no lollygagging, understand? And if I hear anything about you guys taking this van for a joy ride," he stabbed his finger into Patrick's chest, "you're going to be in a lot of trouble. Got it?"

"Yes, sir," Patrick said, winking slyly at Darcy. "Anything you say, Bob."

"Don't get smart with me," Bob said, glowering at Darcy. "That goes for both of you."

"Yes, sir," Darcy replied, his eyes on the ground as he fought to keep from laughing.

They all jumped as an empty pop can hit the ground with a clang. All three of them turned to the bottle cage, where Dean remained hidden, clenching his teeth and his fists in fear of being discovered. Finally, Bob turned back to the delivery boys.

"Probably the wind. Anyway, hurry back. This bottle cage is practically bursting, and I need those cans and bottles sorted before the recycling truck shows up tomorrow morning." His tirade over, he headed back inside.

As soon as their boss was gone, the guys quickly perused the delivery list. "Looks like the usual suspects," Patrick said.

"Oh, man," Darcy groaned. "We got Mrs. Dresden. There's no way I'm going into her place again. Not only does it stink, she's got piles of newspapers stacked all the way to the ceiling. That place is a firetrap."

Patrick grinned at him. "Flip you for it."

Darcy held up his hands and shook his head. "No way. You always win those. How about rock, paper, scissors?"

"You're on."

The boys each put their right fist on the palm of their left hand and then began the chant in unison. "Rock, paper, scissors!"

Darcy smacked his palm with a fist, indicating a rock, and Patrick laid his hand flat, indicating paper.

"Dang it!" Darcy said. "You always win those too!"

"Tell you what," Patrick replied. "Just to be fair, I'll let you deliver to the Dells' place."

At the mention of the name, Dean's ears perked up,

and he peeked around the corner of the bag of bottles as the boys continued to talk.

"Mrs. Dell? Why is she getting a delivery?" Darcy asked. "She's not even old."

"She broke her leg, and she can't get to the store."

Darcy frowned, still not getting it. "So, why would I want to deliver to her?"

"The entire family's going to be there."

"So?"

Patrick shook his head. "You're not listening. The *entire family* is going to be there. They're having a family reunion. That's why they need all these groceries."

Darcy's eyes lit up. "Including Gwen?"

Patrick flicked Darcy's ear. "She's in the family, isn't she? Now come on, this van won't load itself."

As the boys disappeared into the store, Dean pulled out his victim's information sheet and looked at it. The name at the top of the page read, "Gwen Dell." It featured a photo of the blonde with a beautiful smile who had stolen Darcy's heart. Dean had been wondering how he was going to make it all the way to her house undetected, and now he had been presented with a golden opportunity. There was just one problem: if the stock boys discovered him inside the van, they would be sure to report him to their boss—or worse. But that was a chance Dean was willing to take.

Hearing the boys returning, he dashed out of the bottle cage and dove through the van's open sliding door. Without a moment to lose, he spotted some moving blankets piled in a corner and dove underneath them. He had just managed to pull them over his head when the van's rear doors opened, and the boys began loading the groceries. A few minutes later, the rear doors and the sliding door slammed shut, and Dean felt the van rock as the boys got into the front seats. He smiled to himself as the van roared to life and then pulled away from the loading dock. This was going to be way too easy.

In the alley, a pair of eyes watched as the van pulled away. Then a dark hooded figure stepped out of the shadows, jumped onto a bike, and pedaled after it.

§

"Come on, Billy, faster, faster!" Mrs. Muller said, her eyes on a stopwatch as Billy, his face flushed and dripping with sweat, struggled through the makeshift obstacle course she had created in her backyard. It included an old swing set; a mini trampoline; an extension ladder turned into horizontal monkey bars; some worn-out winter tires to run through, like football players do during spring training; four pallets attached together and standing on end as a climbing wall; a balance beam made from scrap lumber; and an alligator crawl constructed out of garden netting attached to several posts stuck into the ground.

"I still . . . don't understand . . . why . . . I need to . . . do this," Billy huffed as he dove under the netting and struggled to crawl forward on his elbows and knees, just like Mrs. Muller had taught him. "We're not going to encounter any barbed wire on our missions, are we?"

"There's no way to know that for certain, Billy," Mrs. Muller replied. "We have to be prepared for anything. Now, less talk, more crawl. Move it, move it!"

Gritting his teeth, Billy dragged himself over the last few feet and then collapsed onto his back, gasping for breath. "How'd I . . . how'd I do this time?"

Mrs. Muller clicked the stopwatch and then shook her head. "Not very good, Billy. Not good at all. In fact, you were two seconds slower than last time. Come on now; on your feet. Let's do it again."

Billy put his hand on his stomach. "I can't, Mrs. Muller, I can't. My stomach hurts, I haven't had anything to eat for hours, and I—"

"Do you want to win this game or not, private?" Mrs. Muller shouted, standing over him.

"Yes, but—"

"Then get up! The more you sweat in training, the less you bleed in battle. Do you want to sweat, Billy, or do you want to bleed?"

Billy sprang to his feet. "Sweat! I want to sweat!"

"Good. Then show me. Go, go, go, go, go!"

She started the stopwatch and then ran alongside him as he started another round, yelling in his ear as he pulled himself across the swing set, using only the chains from the swings to hold himself off the ground. Once across, he jumped down, ran through the tires, hopped onto the mini trampoline, and then sprang up and grabbed the rungs of the extension ladder.

About midway across, his pace started to falter. "I don't think I . . . I don't think I—"

"Don't think, Billy. Do!"

"I'm trying, Mrs. Muller, I'm trying!"

"Do or do not!" she yelled. "There is no try! Haven't you seen Star Wars?"

Clenching his teeth, the cords in his neck sticking out, Billy reached for the next rung. But it was no use. His fingers peeled off, and he hit the ground—hard.

As he lay there, gasping, Mrs. Muller stood over him, one leg on either side of his body. "You know what you are, Billy? You're pathetic. Weak. A worm. Even lower than a worm. You shouldn't be crawling under that barbed wire. You should be tunneling under it, eating dirt. I thought you were stronger than Dean, but I was wrong. You're not worthy to be on my team. You're not even a—"

Before she could utter another word, Billy leaped to his feet and grabbed her by the front of her blouse. "Stop yelling at me!"

Mrs. Muller was so surprised by the sudden attack that she cried out and stumbled backwards. She lost her balance and fell, Billy landing hard on top of her. They hit the ground with a thump, knocking the wind out of Mrs. Muller. As she lay there struggling for breath, it was Billy's turn to stand over her and yell. "I'm done with your stupid training. Do you hear me? Finished! And I'm done with this game. No amount of money is worth what you're putting me through. In fact, you're done too."

Before Mrs. Muller could react, he ran over to the back porch and grabbed her water pistol, pointing it at her as she struggled to her feet.

"What are you going to do, Billy, huh?"

"I'm going to take you out of the game. And then I'm going to take myself out."

"After all we've been through together? You're just going to give up?"

"Yes!"

"Think about it, Billy," Mrs. Muller said, edging closer. "One hundred dollars. Just think of what you can do with all that cash."

Billy wrinkled his brow. "One hundred dollars? I thought the winner gets two hundred and fifty. That means, as your partner, I should get one hundred and twenty-five."

"Well, it is my team, Billy."

Billy tightened his grip on the water pistol as Mrs. Muller crept closer. "Stop right there. It's *our* team, so we split the prize money fifty-fifty, or I pull this trigger. In fact, we split it sixty-forty in my favor and you have to do one round on this obstacle course while I time you."

Mrs. Muller froze in place, knowing Billy had the drop on her. "Okay, but—"

At that moment, the back screen door opened, and Mr. Muller came out with a tray of lemonade and cookies. "Hey, I thought you two might like—"

In a flash, Mrs. Muller twisted Billy's arm behind his back and squeezed until he released the water pistol.

"Ow!" he cried.

Ignoring him, she slipped the pistol into the waistband of her jeans, tucking it under her shirt behind her back. Mr. Muller froze in the doorway, tray in hand, his foot propping the screen door open, and his eyes wide as he stared at his wife. "Audrey, what on earth are you doing?"

Mrs. Muller released Billy and then dusted him off. "Oh, nothing you would understand, Dennis. Just completing Billy's training. You can leave the snacks on the porch. Thank you."

Mr. Muller stood there for a moment, not knowing what to do, but then he followed his wife's instructions and retreated back into the house. He was concerned for Billy, but he knew better than to argue with Audrey when she was in one of her moods.

The moment Dennis was gone, Mrs. Muller pulled the water pistol out of her waistband, grabbed Billy's hand, and slapped the gun into his palm. "It's yours now, private. You've earned it."

Billy stared at the water pistol and then looked up at her in confusion. "What? I thought I—"

"I've been waiting for that killer instinct to surface, and it finally has. Why do you think I've been pushing you so hard? Now drink some lemonade, eat some cookies, and then get yourself home to clean up and get some rest. We've got a big day tomorrow."

"We do?"

Mrs. Muller pulled out another water pistol and checked to make sure it was working properly. "Yup. I plan to take out five people by sundown."

Billy's eyes widened. "Sundown?" Then his face hardened. "By sundown. Got it." He started toward the porch and then turned back. "And thank you, sir—ma'am."

"Don't mention it, Billy. By the way, fifty-fifty it is."

Billy paused for a moment. "But what if we add someone else to our team?"

"Let me deal with that," she replied. "If we do, their share will come out of my half, not yours."

"Deal," Billy said, smiling. Then he shoved his water pistol into his waistband and turned back toward the lemonade and cookies.

14

DOUGHNUTS

Emily knocked on Ben's bedroom door, which was decorated with a poster of a cow head-butting a cowboy out of a corral, along with the slogan, "Mooove it or lose it."

"Ben, are you in there? Moo once if you are and twice if you're not."

The door opened, revealing Ben's scowling face, his bedhead bouncing in the breeze created by the door's movement. "That doesn't even make sense."

"Got you to open the door though, didn't it?" she said, grinning sweetly.

Unimpressed, Ben started to close the door, but Emily blocked it with her foot.

"Not so fast, big brother. I need to talk to you about something."

Ben sighed in frustration. "What?"

"The cow box."

"What about it?"

"Why don't you want to open it?"

"I just don't."

Emily tilted her head sideways and scrunched up her face. "You're not even the least bit curious?"

"Nope."

"Well, I am."

Ben shrugged. "Then too bad for you. Now if you're finished—"

"What if I told you that I know what's in the box?"

Ben relaxed his hold on the doorknob and opened the door a little wider. "Well, do you?"

Emily crossed her arms and shrugged. "Maybe I do, and maybe I don't."

In a flash, Ben whipped the door open and grabbed her by the shoulders. "There's someone inside, isn't there?"

Emily's eyes went wide, frightened at her brother's sudden, uncharacteristic aggression. "M-maybe."

"Did he tell you to get me? To lure me out there?"

Emily frowned. "How did you know it's a he?"

"I didn't—until now. Who is it, and what did he say he would give you?"

Emily lowered her eyes to the carpet, her lower lip sticking out. "Candy. Lots and lots of candy. But now that you know the secret, I won't get any."

"Wait a second," Ben said. "What if I made you an even better offer?"

Emily tilted her head up to look at him, a flicker of hope in her glistening blue eyes. "A better offer? To do what?"

Ben grinned and then released her shoulders and opened his bedroom door, beckoning her to enter. "Come on inside. I think I have a plan."

§

Just Dean's luck, the Dells' house was the last stop on the grocery van's delivery route. In addition to being jostled and bumped around for forty-five minutes due to the van's crummy rear suspension and Patrick's erratic driving, it was sweltering under the moving blankets, and

Dean was sweating buckets. It was all he could do to keep his target away from his chest to prevent it from getting soaked. He was also getting terribly carsick.

"You know what?" Patrick said, checking his watch. "We're ahead of schedule. Want to make one quick stop before we go to the Dells' place?"

"Aw, can't we just get it over with?" Darcy asked. "My stomach has been in knots the entire time just thinking about seeing Gwen again." Gwen was from Saskatoon, but each summer, she came to stay with her cousin, Pam, and her family for a few weeks, which was how she had become involved in Assassin. Although Darcy had liked Gwen for the past few summers, he was still working up the nerve to ask her out.

"Just for a few minutes," Patrick said. "It'll be fun."

"Well, where do you want to go?"

Patrick looked at Darcy and grinned. "You'll see."

In the back of the van, Dean groaned.

Patrick whipped his head back toward the cargo area. "What was that?"

Beneath the moving blankets, Dean went rigid, trying to remain as stationary and as silent as possible.

Darcy looked back and then turned forward again, rubbing his belly. "Probably my stomach. I'm starving. Let's step on it."

Patrick nailed the gas, and Dean did his best to hold on—and to keep from throwing up.

§

Out on his first solo patrol since arriving in Milligan Creek, Constable Link couldn't help but smile to himself as he reveled in his newfound freedom. It was a hot day, and he could have put on the air conditioning, but he decided to roll down the windows instead, which made it easier to stay in touch with the community he was committed to serve and protect.

He waved at a couple of seniors standing in front of the bulletin board outside the Co-op store, and one of them waved back. Constable Link sighed with contentment. This really was the quintessential small town, where everyone knew everyone and nothing dark or seedy ever went on beneath the surface. It was a pity the RCMP's policy was to move officers every few years. He could envision spending the rest of his life there: getting married, raising a family, and watching his kids grow up safe and secure as they walked the streets of Milligan Creek, just like the little girl he spotted pulling her doll in a red wagon down the sidewalk. He waved to her, and she smiled and waved back. Ah, yes, a man could get used to living in a place like this . . ..

§

As soon as the patrol car was out of sight, the little girl—Emily—shoved her doll aside and pulled out a stack of posters and a roll of tape. She slapped a poster onto a lamppost and then taped it in place before moving on. A careful observer would have noted a string of such posters affixed to lampposts, railings, and store windows all the way down Main Street—all the way to the bulletin board outside the Co-op grocery store.

§

"It's a kidnapping, I tell ya," old Tom Pew insisted as he stared at the poster outside the Co-op. It featured a photo of Ian and offered information regarding his location in return for a ransom. It also included a phone number. All of it was written in purple pencil crayon.

"Why don't you call the police?" asked Howard Long, Tom's neighbor and verbal sparring partner since high school. Both men had long since retired from farming and moved to town. Now they spent most of their days bickering on the bench outside the Co-op or swapping tales, drinking coffee, and playing cards and checkers with the other retirees in the seniors' center down the street.

"Are you kidding me?" Tom said. "The police are probably in on it."

Howard stared at his friend in disbelief and then waved his hand in dismissal. "Bah, you're always looking for a devil behind every bush." He sat back down on the bench and rested his hands on the top of his cane as he watched the cars drive by. "Besides, that's the Spencer boy, isn't it? What person in their right mind would ever pay a ransom to get him back? I'm surprised it's not a poster with his parents offering money to anybody who'll take him off their hands."

Tom scratched his grizzled chin and pushed back his tweed newsboy hat as he stared at the poster. Then he ripped it off the bulletin board and shuffled down the street.

"Hey, where are you going?" Howard called after him. "I thought we were going to play checkers!"

"Checkers can wait!" Tom replied, waving the poster in the air. "I've got a mystery to solve!"

Howard shook his head in frustration and then settled back on the bench.

"Good afternoon, Mr. Long," Emily said as she passed by with her wagon, having completed her mission.

"Bah, what's good about it?" Howard asked.

The moment his eyes were fixed back on the street, Emily stuck another poster on the bulletin board and then disappeared around the corner—just as the Co-op delivery van pulled up to the stop sign beside her.

Inside the van, Darcy sank low in his seat. "Careful! You want Bob to see us?"

"Relax," Patrick said, looking both ways before he pulled through the intersection. "Bob's probably back in his office with his feet up on his desk talking to his girlfriend on the phone, just like he does every day. Besides, we're almost there."

After crossing Main Street, they drove for another few blocks until they reached a large vacant area, the former site of the town's elementary school. Now it was where the school buses were kept for the summer. About twenty of them were parked in a semi-circle around the perimeter of the lot under some towering elm trees, preventing anyone outside the lot from seeing what was going on inside.

Patrick made sure no one was around and then grinned at Darcy. "Hang on!" He punched the accelerator to the floor and cranked the steering wheel.

"Whoo-hoo!" Darcy exclaimed, clutching the door handle as the van's rear tires sprayed gravel and the vehicle spun around in a circle, sending up a cloud of dust as they made doughnuts in the vacant lot.

In the back of the van, Dean held on for dear life as the bags and boxes of groceries slid to one side of the van, vegetables, fruit, cans, and bottles spilling everywhere. Then Patrick cranked the steering wheel the other way, pedal to the metal, and everything slid to the other side of the van. Dean barely managed to hold on to a hook on the wall of the van—and his lunch.

Finally, Patrick eased off the gas, straightened out the steering wheel, and set off toward their next destination. At that point, assassinating his target was the last thing on Dean's mind. All he wanted to do was get out of that van.

He got his wish a few minutes later when the vehicle lurched to a stop. The van rocked as Patrick and Darcy got out. The side door flew open. Now all Dean had to do was wait until the boys took the groceries inside the house, and then he could make his escape.

"Man, look at this mess!" Darcy exclaimed. "How're we going to know whose groceries are whose? Everything's scattered everywhere. And look at these peaches. They're all bruised," he added, holding up a clear cellophane bag. "I told you we should have waited until after we were finished our route."

"Whatever. Grab the list," Patrick ordered. "I'm sure we can sort things out."

Under the moving blankets, Dean clutched his stomach in agony. Sort things out? He didn't think he—or his insides—could wait that long.

"Here's the list," Darcy said, returning to Patrick's side. "I don't know how much help it'll be though. All it has is a list of names and addresses."

"Not that list, dummy," Patrick said, handing it back. "The other one, the one we used to fill their orders."

"Oh, I left that back at the store," Darcy replied, scratching his head. "I didn't think we'd need it."

Patrick sighed. "Great. Now we have to—" Before he could finish his sentence, a movement in the corner of the van caught his eye. "What the . . .?"

Suddenly, the moving blankets flew to the side, revealing Dean, his face white and his eyes bulging out of their sockets. "Outta my way!"

He charged forward, but before he could jump out of the van, they grabbed him, each boy gripping one of his upper arms with fists of steel.

"A stowaway, hey?" Patrick said, his face menacing as he leaned in so close that Dean could smell his breath. Black

105

licorice. Gross. Dean hated black licorice. "Hey, Darcy, what did Bob tell us to do if we ever found a stowaway?"

"I don't remember," Darcy said, pressing his face in close to Dean's as he squeezed his arm even harder, "but I'm sure we can come up with something."

"I'd let me go if I were you," Dean warned.

Darcy scoffed. "Oh yeah? Or else what?"

"Or else . . ." Dean swallowed hard. "Or else . . . *bleeeeech!*"

Patrick looked on in horror as Dean threw up all over Darcy's clothes, his shoes, and his face.

15

A CONSPIRACY UNMASKED

"Hello, anybody home?"

Emily rapped her knuckles on the side of the "cow box," as she had taken to calling it.

"Yes, I'm still in here," Ian growled. "Where else would I be?"

Emily clasped her hands in front of her waist and smiled. "Just checking."

"So, what's up with Ben? Have you figured out how to get him here? I can't wait all day. It's hot inside this box, and I'm getting thirsty. And I need to go to the bathroom."

"Don't worry; he should be along shortly," Emily said, glancing out the window. She turned back to the box and pulled a piece of paper out of her pocket. "By the way, I've made a list of all the candy I want once this is over."

"Fine, whatever," Ian replied. "Just get your brother in here!"

§

Hunched over his green Arborite-and-chrome kitchen table with his reading glasses on, Tom Pew slid a ruler down the pages of the Milligan Creek phone book as he scrutinized each number, looking for a match with the one on the ransom poster. His tweed hat hung from the back of his chair, the crown of his bald, surprisingly white head glistening in the light of the desk lamp beside him. Though a lifelong bachelor, he was meticulous about housekeeping. His kitchen, like the rest of his house, was spotless.

"Bingo!" he exclaimed, sitting back so suddenly that he knocked his hat to the floor. His orange cat, Chester, who had been lazing on the table beside him, raised his head for a moment out of curiosity and then laid back down. "I knew I recognized that number from somewhere!" Tom said.

He turned off the lamp and put his reading glasses back into their case. Then he set the case in its proper place on the table—perfectly parallel to his placemat. "Don't wait up for me, Chester," he said, scratching the cat behind the ears, causing it to arch its back in pleasure. Then Tom pushed back his chair, scooped up his hat, and headed for the door as fast as his old legs would carry him.

§

Darcy clutched Dean's arm, vomit dripping from his face and his clothes, not knowing whether to let the boy go or punch him in the face. Then the smell hit him, and his own stomach lurched.

"Oh, man," Patrick said, stifling a laugh. "If only I had a camera right now."

"Shut up," Darcy snarled. "You wouldn't be laughing if it happened to you."

"Probably not," Patrick said, "but it's still funny."

Darcy used the back of his free hand to wipe his face as he glared at Dean. "You're in a lot of trouble, kid. Just wait till I—"

Dean's eyes went wide as he spotted something behind

his captors. "Look out!" he cried.

Darcy scoffed. "Oldest trick in the book. You really think I'm going to fall for that?"

"I mean it," Dean replied. "Look out!"

Before Darcy could react, Dean wrenched free from their grasp and scrunched into a ball, pulling his arms and legs into his chest.

"What the—" Darcy turned around just in time to be hit full in the face with a blast of water from a garden hose. He held up his arms to block it, but the water kept coming, drenching him and Patrick, who was also trying to shield himself from the onslaught.

"Stop it already!" Patrick cried. "What the heck?"

Finally, the water died away. As the stock boys wiped their eyes, they heard the van's rear doors open.

"The stowaway!" Darcy yelled, momentarily forgetting their assailant, who they had yet to identify due to the barrage of water.

The boys ran around to the back of the van, but by the time they got there, Dean had already hurdled a hedge and disappeared into the neighbor's backyard. When they turned back toward the Dells' house, all they saw was the hose lying on the ground. Whoever had sprayed them was nowhere in sight.

"What was that all about?" Patrick asked.

"I don't know, but look at these groceries," Darcy said, gesturing to the van's interior, which was dripping with water. "They're soaked! How are we going to explain this?"

"We'll tell Bob the truth—we had just discovered a stowaway when we were attacked," Patrick said, coming up beside him. "And look on the bright side: with all that water, at least you won't smell so bad on the ride back to the store."

Darcy looked down at his sopping wet clothes, which

were almost vomit free. "Yeah, I guess you're right," he agreed, wringing out his shirt.

Just as they were about to get back into the van, the front door opened, and Pam and Gwen stepped out. "Are you here with our groceries?" Pam asked.

Gwen did a double-take as she took a closer look at the boys. "Why are you soaking wet?"

Darcy opened his mouth to reply when both girls pinched their nostrils shut and Gwen waved her hand in front of her face. "Ugh, what's that smell?"

Patrick took a step away from Darcy and tilted his head toward him, pointing to indicate that Darcy was the source of the smell. Darcy picked up on the silent message and held up his hands in protest.

"It's not me, Gwen! I swear!"

"Yuck, I can't stand it anymore!" Pam turned and ran into the house, followed by Gwen.

When the girls were gone, Darcy turned to Patrick in a rage. "Thanks for backing me up, buddy."

"Don't blame me. Blame the kid who puked on you. Now come on; we need to get back to the store and get this sorted out."

Darcy took a final look at the house and then sighed. So much for making a good first impression.

Crouched behind some bushes next door, Dean waited until the delivery van drove away. Only then did he dare look down at the target on his chest. By some miracle, it was still dry, and he was still in the game!

Elated at having survived his near-death experience, Dean peeked out of the bushes at Pam's house. His would-be assassin was nowhere in sight. He wished he had been able to catch a glimpse of the person's face, but whoever it was had been wearing a hoodie. Dean had been so sick, and everything had happened so fast that the person's face didn't register.

He checked his watch. He still had plenty of daylight. Figuring he was in as good a place as any, he pulled out his water pistol and hunkered down to wait for his quarry to emerge from the house.

§

Ben sat on a kitchen chair beneath his family's wall-mounted phone waiting for it to ring. He looked at the clock. The posters had been up for a couple of hours already. Whoever was supposed to assassinate the person in the box would have to see one sooner or later. Unless that person was so afraid of getting assassinated that he or she was hunkered down at home, just like Ben.

Speaking of which, what was he doing waiting by the phone? He should be out stalking his target. Trying to set a trap for his would-be killer was a waste of time. Instead of sitting around waiting for someone to call, this was the perfect opportunity to go after his own victim, knowing there was no one chasing him. In return for a bit more candy, he could have Emily keep an eye on the box and then alert him whenever Ian came out. Meanwhile, he would be able to add another kill to his list.

Ben stood up. But just as he was about to go out and tell Emily his new plan, two things happened. First, the phone rang, nearly causing Ben to have a cow, so to speak. Then, as he reached out to answer it, he saw a flash of something outside the window. It looked like . . . tweed.

Ben froze, his hand on the receiver. Could his killer have gotten out of the box? If so, why hadn't Emily come to warn him? Unless . . . unless the killer had made another deal with her. If so, Ben was going to have some pretty strong words for her. Imagine that, his own sister betraying him twice in one day!

The phone continued to ring, and Ben continued to waffle. He tried to get a better look out the window, but no one was in sight. He was just beginning to think his mind was playing tricks on him when he heard the distinctive sound of footsteps on the back porch. He looked at the clock again. It was too early for his parents to be home from running errands. The question was, had they locked the back door? He looked down the hall to see if the deadbolt was open or closed, but it was too dark to tell.

The phone rang again. He knew if he didn't answer it now, he might miss out on a golden opportunity to take out his assassin. Finally, he picked up the receiver, his eyes still on the back door.

"H-hello?"

§

Tom hunkered down in the hollyhocks alongside Ben's house, pulling his tweed cap low over his eyes, so it would be harder to recognize him. His old heart was beating faster than it had in years. He was elated. After years of suspecting dark and nefarious things were going on beneath the surface of the supposedly sleepy, peaceful little town of Milligan Creek, he finally had proof. And if he saved the Spencer boy, he would be a hero. He could already imagine his triumphant entry into the seniors' center once the story broke in the news. Howard would be the first person to apologize—or more likely the last; he was such a stubborn old fool. The women at the seniors' center would be a different story. Perhaps Tom wouldn't have to end his life as a lonely bachelor after all . . ..

The question was, where was the Spencer boy being held? No one was home but the Somerville's cow-obsessed kid, and he was just sitting like a dunce by the phone in the kitchen. There was no way he could be in on the caper. Unless . . . that was it! The kids *were* in on it, probably forced by their parents to participate in the nefarious scheme. If so, where were the parents holding the Spencer boy? Tom had already peeked in every window, and the single-story house didn't have a basement. That meant the kidnappers could only be in one place.

§

Emily was sitting on her father's greasy, tool-covered workbench in the garage and had nearly nodded off when she saw something out the window. It was Ben. He was jumping up and down and waving to get her attention. He pointed to the garage's overhead door and then mimicked her pushing the button to open it. She gave him a thumbs-up and then slid down off the workbench. She was elated. No matter how things went down, she was going to get a candy payday.

"Okay, he's outside," she said to Ian. "I'm going to open the overhead door to let in some light. The minute you hear Ben's voice, jump out of the box, and you'll get him for sure."

"It's about time!" Ian said. "Good work, by the way."

Emily smiled as she reached for the button. "Thanks! Here goes nothin'!"

The door's electric motor clicked and then made a grinding noise, as if it were barely strong enough for the job. As the door inched up, Emily's heart raced, and she rubbed her hands together in anticipation. All she could think about was candy. Lots and lots of candy. But as the door rose further, she frowned. Instead of revealing Ian's assassin, it revealed the legs of a spindly old man in a tweed hat, Tom Pew, who was holding Ben in a headlock as the boy struggled to break free.

"Close the door, Emily. Close the door!" Ben cried out. "There's been a terrible misunderstanding!"

Emily's eyes flew to the cow box, which was rocking back and forth as Ian struggled to pop it open. Little did he realize his older teenage brother, who had sealed Ian inside and dropped him off on the Somervilles' front porch hours earlier, had applied extra tape as a joke to foil Ian's assassination attempt.

"Don't touch that button, little girl," Tom warned. "You two are in enough trouble as it is."

"But you don't understand," Ben said. "I've been trying to tell you, we're just playing a game, and—"

At that moment, the box gave a final rock and then fell over, bursting open. Emily stumbled backwards in fear, her hand slipping off the garage door button as Ian leaped to his feet, let out a yell, and charged out of the garage, a water pistol in each hand.

"Prepare to die!"

16

DOUBLE WHAMMY

Tom was so startled by Ian's sudden appearance that he instinctively released Ben, who dove out of the way just in time to avoid Ian's double-barreled barrage. Tom wasn't as fast on his feet, so he took the deluge of water right in the face. As Ian came to his senses, realizing he had just hosed down an old man instead of Ben, he heard something above. He looked up just in time to take a bucket of cold water full in the face.

"Whoo-hoo!" Matt cried, doing a little dance on the peak of the garage roof and waving the bucket with joy. "Nailed him!"

He tossed the bucket to the ground and then slid down the side of the garage roof and hopped down to the ground, a distance of only about eight feet.

"That was awesome!" Ben said, running up. "Nicely played, Emily." He gave her a high five.

"Yeah, nicely played, Emily," Matt said, also giving her a high five. Then he pulled out his water pistol and shot Ben in the chest.

Ben looked down at his target in shock. "But . . . but . . . why did you do that?"

"Simple," Matt said, walking up to Ian and holding

out his hand. Ian reluctantly surrendered his target and his victim's information. "The minute I took out Ian, that made you my next target, so this is a proverbial case of killing two birds with one stone."

"Don't forget about my candy," Emily reminded him.

Matt smiled. "Don't worry, Emily. You'll get it. Lots of it."

Ben looked at his sister, his face a mixture of surprise, anger, and disappointment. "You betrayed me . . . for him?"

"It was either him or Ian," Emily replied. "I knew you didn't have enough money to get me all of the candy on my list."

"But I'm your brother!"

Emily shrugged. "All's fair in love and war, Ben. You know that." Matt had fed her that line, anticipating such a response from Ben.

At that moment, Tom, who had been watching the exchange in fascination, finally spoke up. "Hold on a second, so there hasn't been a kidnapping?"

All three children looked at him. "No," Matt said. "As Ben tried to tell you, we're just playing a game."

"And I'm really sorry I shot you in the face," Ian added. "I was going for Ben."

"Don't worry about it," Tom said, still dabbing his face with a blue polka-dot hankie, something he never went anywhere without. "Just tell me, what kind of game is it?"

The kids looked at each other uncertainly. They were sworn to secrecy, but Tom knew so much already, there wasn't much they could do.

"It's called Assassin," Matt said, "but that's all we can tell you for now. And please, don't tell anyone else. It's supposed to be for kids only. If our parents find out, they'll shut us down."

Tom thought about it for a moment, and then his eyes narrowed. "You mean I'm the only adult in town who knows what's going on?"

"You and one other," Matt said. "But she promised to keep it a secret too. Please, Mr. Pew. We're having so much fun; we don't want it to end now."

"A real-life conspiracy, hey?" Tom said, a smile creeping across his face. "In Milligan Creek no less."

Matt shrugged. "Yeah, I guess you could call it that."

Tom broke into a grin. "Then it's a deal. Your secret is safe with me."

With those words, he turned and headed down the street. If the kids didn't know any better, they would have said he was skipping.

In truth, Tom couldn't wait to get back to the seniors' center to gloat amongst Howard and the others. He may not have solved a crime, but his longstanding suspicion about Milligan Creek had finally been confirmed. There was more going on beneath the surface of that small town than most people realized, much more. And the only adult—well, the only senior citizen—who knew about it was Tom. He couldn't have been happier.

Back at the garage, Matt walked over to Ben, who was still fuming at his sister's betrayal. "Your target, please." Ben ripped it off his chest and slapped it into Matt's hand. Matt wiggled the fingers of his other hand. "And your victim's information."

As Ben dug into his pocket, a sudden wave of paranoia swept over Matt. He had been so euphoric over the double assassination that he had completely forgotten that someone was hunting him too. "Hurry," he said, peeking over his shoulder. "I need to keep moving."

Finally, Ben found it. Matt snatched it out of his hand and then ran off.

"Hey, what about my candy?" Emily asked.

"I'll leave it for you tomorrow in Dean's garage!" Matt replied over his shoulder.

"I still can't believe it," Ben said, stalking back toward the house. "My own sister."

"Yeah, thanks, Emily," Ian said, walking off in the other direction. "Thanks for nothing."

Emily grinned to herself. She knew they would both get over it, eventually.

§

By the time Dean heard Pam's front door open, he thought he was dreaming. But as he rubbed his eyes and shook his head to clear it, sure enough, he was awake. And even though it was getting dark, there was no mistaking his target's identity. Her blond hair and bright smile were a dead giveaway.

The problem was, Gwen wasn't alone. She was with her grandmother and Pam, who was also playing the game. What if Pam was his assassin? It would make sense, seeing as he had been ambushed outside her house, but how could Pam have known he was in the van? In fact, how could anyone have known he was in the van? It hadn't occurred to him to wonder about that before. Now that he did think about it, the answer was simple. He had been spotted getting into the van and then followed.

That got Pam off the hook, but if his assassin had been following him, had he or she put two and two together and realized Gwen was his target? If so, what if Dean's assassin was also lurking somewhere in the lengthening shadows, just waiting for him to make his move? As Dean saw the threesome heading toward their car, he realized it was a risk he would have to take.

"It sure was nice of you to offer to take us out for ice cream, Grandma," Gwen said. "I just hope it's not too late for you."

"Too late? For ice cream? Never!" her grandmother replied as she pulled her keys out of her purse. She paused when she heard a foot scrape on the gravel behind her. She and the two girls turned, but no one was there.

"Quick! Get in the car!" Pam cried.

"What? What's going on?" her grandmother asked.

"Just hurry!" Gwen said. "Here, give me the keys."

"It's too late, Gwen," Dean said, stepping out of the shadows, holding his water pistol in both hands like he had seen private detectives do on TV shows. "Prepare to—"

Before Dean could finish, he turned tail and ran.

Seconds later, a dark shadow sped past, followed by two more, almost bowling Pam and Gwen's grandmother over. She reached for the car's door handle to steady herself. "Land's sakes! Can somebody tell me what the heck is going on?"

Pam and Gwen looked at each other in fear, not knowing what to say. "That boy has a crush on Gwen!" Pam said finally.

"He does?" their grandmother asked. She huffed as she straightened out her dress. "Well, he sure has a funny way of showing it. Back in my day, if a boy liked you, he would yank on your pigtail or shove you to the ground in the schoolyard, not threaten to shoot you with a water gun in the dead of night."

"Well, times have changed, Grandma," Gwen said, opening the passenger door.

"Yeah, thank goodness," Pam said as she got into the back seat.

Dean ran faster than he had ever run in his life. He vaulted over fences and bushes, dodged in and out of backyards and back alleys, even knocking over garbage cans to slow down his pursuers—another technique he had learned from watching cop shows on TV.

But no matter how fast he ran or what strategy he employed, the people hunting him just got closer, and more numerous. It seemed like the sound of running footsteps was everywhere, streaming toward him from every direction. Whoever was chasing him must have gotten a lot of kills, taking players who had been eliminated onto their team, until a veritable army was chasing Dean through the darkening moonless night.

To make matters worse, a cold front was moving in, causing a fog to settle over the town, which was normally unheard of at that time of year, further obstructing his vision. Twice Dean had stumbled and nearly fallen, which would have meant game over, but each time he recovered, and ran. His only comfort was that if he couldn't see his pursuers, that meant they couldn't see him. If only he could find a place to hide long enough for them to run past. Then he could double back and sneak home—unless they had someone posted at his house as well!

Despite the adrenaline coursing through his body, he felt his pace slowing. It was only a matter of time before his lungs or his legs finally gave out. He passed the sign for his high school and veered to the right. Perhaps he could lose them by weaving through the various utility buildings around back. Or maybe he could even make it onto the school roof. No one would think to look for him up there.

As if anticipating such a move, he heard one of his pursuers swing right, so Dean took a hard left. He was running out of options—and breath. He passed a set of bleachers and ran onto the football field. As he stumbled across the fifty-yard line, his legs finally gave out, and he fell to his knees, gasping for air. He tried to get up but then fell down again.

"Okay, okay," he said, raising his hands—and his water pistol. "I surrender!"

As he knelt there, panting, several dark figures wearing hoodies and sunglasses emerged from the gloom, forming a semi-circle around him. But instead of shooting him, they just stood there, silent.

"Come on, what are you waiting for?" Dean cried. "Just get it over with!" He closed his eyes in anticipation of a barrage of water, but nothing came. And when he opened his eyes again, the dark figures were gone.

Dean shook his head. Had he been dreaming the entire time after all? In reality, was he still hunkered down in the bushes by Pam's house, fast asleep?

But no, the wet, prickly grass on his knees wasn't a dream. Neither were his burning lungs or his screaming thighs, which were already beginning to cramp. But if this wasn't a dream, then what was going on? Had he been so paranoid that he had imagined his pursuers?

Just as Dean was trying to sort it all out in his mind, he heard a strange hissing sound. He looked around in confusion. What was that?

Then, through the gloom, he saw something small and black pop out of the ground in front of him, followed by several more up and down the football field. Only too late did he realize what they were.

Sprinklers.

"Noooooo!"

17

BOUNTIES

The Mullers' garage door rose slowly, revealing Joyce, who squinted in the early morning light as she organized the table where players would turn in bounties and pick up new equipment to help their cause. Business had been steady over the past few days, and pickings were slim. Only a couple of umbrellas, a bucket, and a few mediocre water guns remained. She was just settling into her chair when Matt raced through the doorway and skidded to a stop in front of the table.

"Morning, Joyce!" he said, smiling as he handed in his bounties from the day before.

"Nice work," Joyce replied, scooping them up. "Care to upgrade your weapon?" She gestured to the items on the table. "Or are you still taking the purist route?"

"Well, to be honest, I did improvise yesterday. With a bucket. But everyone's allowed at least one exception."

"Fair enough," Joyce replied. "By the way, where did you sleep you last night? Mom and Dad are really starting to wonder why you're on such an exercise kick lately."

Inspired by a news story he had read about the famed Colombian drug trafficker, Pablo Escobar, Matt had taken to sleeping in a different undisclosed location each night, so as to avoid being taken out by his enemies. To pull it off, he faked an early bedtime, claiming he had to get up early to go for a long run in preparation for an upcoming marathon, and then snuck out his window. Sometimes he slept in the tree house—which he had rigged with a zipline that would allow him to escape in the event his pursuers came up the ladder—and other times he slept in his parents' vehicles or hidden in the workshop. To switch things up, he had spent the previous night in his father's two-seater Cessna airplane. Never again. The seats were terribly uncomfortable, and the stench of the decaying vinyl upholstery almost made him sick.

All the subterfuge was necessary now though, seeing as Chad was on Fiona's team, and he had refused to declare a truce when the brothers were inside the home. As a result, Matt and Chad hadn't been in the house at the same time for the past few days, another thing that was causing their parents to become suspicious—that and the fact Chad had taken to wearing his black sunglasses day and night.

"I'm sorry, but that's classified," Matt said. "I realize you're supposed to be impartial, but as they say, loose lips sink ships."

"Whatever," Joyce said as more players approached the garage, some trudging in defeat, their shoulders slouched, and others racing like a tsunami wave was at their heels. "Just don't blame me when you get busted."

Matt stood to the side as the garage filled up with kids. They created a cacophony of noise, some players turning in their bounties and others disputing the legitimacy of their "death."

"It's not fair," one girl, Stacey, complained. "I was going through our weekly car wash with my dad yesterday when Greg popped out of hiding in the back seat and hit the button to roll down my window. Not only did I get soaked, my dad grounded me for sneaking a boy into the car—and it wasn't even my fault!"

"I'm sorry, Stacey," Joyce replied, "but Greg cleared the car wash idea with me yesterday."

"Hmph," Stacey replied, slapping her target on the table. "Well, no one cleared it with me." She walked away in a huff.

"Moo."

Joyce smiled as Ben shuffled into the garage. "How's it going, Ben?"

"Not good."

"You out of the game?"

He nodded. "It was an 'udder' catastrophe."

"No, it wasn't," Matt replied. "It was brilliant! I'll have to tell you all about it later, Joyce. That reminds me." He pulled a bag out of his backpack and held it out to Ben. "Do you mind giving this to Emily?"

Ben looked at it and then turned away and sniffed. "Not a chance."

Matt shrugged, then set it on the table. "She'll come by for it sometime later today, Joyce."

"You going to wait around to see if someone picks you up for their team?" Joyce asked Ben.

He nodded. "Yup."

She smiled. "Well, I don't think you'll have to wait long." She gestured toward the door. Ben and the other kids, including Matt, turned to see what she was looking at. Their eyes were met by a line of players, all of them wearing black sunglasses, just like their leader, Fiona. She stepped up to the table, a stack of bounties in hand.

"Wow! Looks like you had a busy night," Joyce said, taking them from her.

"You could say that." Fiona turned to Matt and smiled.

"How was your night, Matt? Feeling . . . airsick?"

Matt was about to respond, but then his eyes went wide. "What? How did you—" Then a cold wave of realization washed over his face and into his gut, chilling his insides. He looked at his brother. "You . . . you've been spying on me!"

Chad grinned. "Have to, little brother. Need to keep track of you in preparation for the day when we finally find you in our sights."

Matt scoffed. "In your dreams. Besides, the way you're going, even if your team wins—and that's a big if—you'll be lucky to get a couple of bucks out of the deal."

"Plus bragging rights," Andrew reminded him.

"That's right," Chad said, nodding. "You can't put a price on that."

"Oh yes you can," Matt replied. "Two hundred and fifty dollars, to be exact, and it's all going straight to me."

"Cool your jets, boys," Joyce said. Then she turned to Fiona and gestured to the equipment table. "So, what'll it be? Better guns? A bucket? Some umbrellas?"

"I'll just take some more sunglasses," Fiona said, holding out her hand. "Seven pairs. That is, if you still have any left in my color." She grinned at Matt. He turned away, shaking his head in disgust.

"Oh, we have plenty," Joyce replied, reaching under the table and pulled out a plastic grocery bag. "I actually ran out and bought some extra pairs yesterday in anticipation of this." She and Fiona grinned at Matt, but he wouldn't meet their gaze.

"Excellent." Fiona took them from her. Then she turned to examine the group of victims who had assembled in the garage alongside the people who had taken them out. "Now, who should I choose to go on my team?"

"Pick me! Pick me!" a chorus of voices cried.

"No, pick me!" a chubby boy named Vince said, running up to the garage.

"But you're not even dead yet," Chad said, pointing at his unblemished target.

Without hesitation, Vince pulled out his water pistol and shot himself in the chest. "Now I am! See?" He ripped off his dripping target and held it up.

Fiona curled her upper lip, unimpressed. "Thanks, but no thanks."

Vince's face fell. "What? But why?"

"Anyone that desperate to join my team shouldn't be on my team."

Horror-struck, Vince stared at his target. "But that means . . . that means I just did that . . . for nothing?"

"Hand it over," Joyce said. "I'll need your victim's information too."

"Excellent," Mrs. Muller said, entering through the side door with Billy in tow. "Vince was our first target for the day."

She and Billy did a high five, and then Joyce handed her the information sheet for Vince's victim.

Mrs. Muller looked at the group and grinned. "Why all the long faces? This is a great day to be alive, isn't that right, Billy?"

"Yup," Billy replied, his face like granite behind his pink neon sunglasses. He and Mrs. Muller did another high five.

As they celebrated, Dean sidled in the door, his eyes downcast and his hands deep in his pockets.

"Well, well, well," Mrs. Muller said. "If it isn't my long-lost son."

"No way," Matt exclaimed. "Who got you?"

Dean looked at Fiona and her sunglass-clad crew. "Who do you think?"

Fiona approached Dean with a pair of sunglasses. "Don't feel bad, Dean. You're part of the family now. By the way, that's three down, one to go." She grinned at Matt.

"Dean, don't do it!" Matt said. "You can't join her team too!"

"What else am I supposed to do?" Dean asked in despair. "Join yours?"

Matt's shoulders slumped slightly. "I don't have a team." His face hardened as he looked at Fiona. "And I'm still not forming one."

Fiona smiled and held the sunglasses out to Dean. "These are going to look great on you."

Just as Dean was about to take them, Mrs. Muller knocked his hand away. "Not so fast!" She shoved a pair of pink neon sunglasses into his hand. "Join Billy and me instead."

Dean turned the pink sunglasses over in his hands and then looked up at his mother in surprise. "You want *me* to join *your* team?"

"You're my son, aren't you?"

Dean crossed his arms. "I thought you said it was too late for me; that I was going to show up here with my target soaked and my tail tucked between my legs."

"Well, no offense, but you kind of did that today," Mrs. Muller said, glancing at Billy, who chuckled and nodded. He had become a prototypical yes man. "But once you complete my training, you'll be transformed. Isn't that right, Billy?"

Billy crossed his arms, put on his toughest expression, and nodded. "Yup."

Dean looked at Billy in disgust. "You think I want to turn out like him?" He scoffed. "Keep your sunglasses." He tossed them back to his mother. "I already have a pair." He held out his hand to Fiona. "If you'd be so kind."

Smiling, Fiona handed him a pair of black sunglasses.

"You're making a good choice, Dean."

"No, you're making a big mistake," Mrs. Muller warned him.

"We'll see about that," Dean said, slipping on his sunglasses and joining the lineup of Fiona's minions. He pulled out his water pistol and crossed his arms, trying to look as tough as possible.

Matt shook his head as he surveyed Fiona's growing army. He and his friends had started the game to get kids away from her, but people were still being drawn to her like flies to rotten meat, including Matt's closest friends. What was it about the girl that made everyone lose their minds, and how was it that Matt appeared to be the only person who was immune? It was like Fiona had the entire town hypnotized.

He was yanked out of his thoughts when a girl came running up to the garage, breathless.

"Rhonda, what's going on?" Joyce asked. "Is someone chasing you?"

"No!" Rhonda replied, struggling to catch her breath. "Haven't you heard the news?"

"What news?" Matt asked, stepping forward. "Has someone blown the cover on our game?"

"No! They've just announced the winner of the Miss Milligan Creek contest!"

"And . . .?" Joyce asked, gesturing for Rhonda to continue. "Who won?"

Rhonda grinned. "Who do you think? Ladies and gentlemen," she said, extending her arms dramatically toward Fiona, "I give you . . . Miss Milligan Creek!"

As everyone gathered around Fiona to congratulate her, Matt smacked himself in the forehead. She really had mesmerized the entire town.

129

18

A LATE-NIGHT OFFER

Following the announcement of Fiona's impending coronation, the rest of the day saw a fresh outbreak of assassinations, each one more daring and creative than the one before as the remaining players vied for top spot. Something about the upcoming Milligan Creek Daze celebrations, which were to take place the following day, lent a new feeling of urgency to the game. Everyone seemed to sense that when the big day arrived, with it would come the end of the competition—that and they knew it would be difficult to enjoy any of the events if they had to spend the entire time worrying about an assassin trying to take them out.

Mrs. Muller and Billy started on a roll, taking out four targets in quick succession. Their first victim went down at the library due to a rigged drinking fountain. Billy and Mrs. Muller had increased the likelihood of him taking a drink by cranking the library's thermostat until it was sweltering. It nearly caused the librarian to get heatstroke, but it got the job done.

Their second victim "died" in the produce section of the Co-op. One second, she was reaching for a head of butter lettuce, and the next second, she and the other customers found themselves surrounded by a cloud of mist, the produce cooler's sprinkler system having suddenly "malfunctioned."

"Dang it, Patrick!" Bob said as he tried to readjust the nozzles. "Have you been messing with this thing again?"

The assassination of their third victim was a bit more elaborate. Bold as brass, Billy walked up to the person's front door and rang the doorbell. When he spotted his target through the screen door, he raced inside, flushing him out the back. As their victim bounded off the back porch, instead of landing on the metal steps, he stumbled and fell into two feet of water. Mrs. Muller had borrowed her husband's socket set to unbolt the steps from the wall overnight and replaced them with a blow-up kiddie pool.

Their fourth victim went down at a softball practice while preparing for the annual Milligan Creek Daze tournament. Desperate for a drink after running bases in the sweltering heat, she reached for a Gatorade bottle, only to have the lid pop off as she tipped it up for a drink, soaking her. (Billy had crept in and loosened the caps on all the Gatorade bottles prior to practice.)

With only one victim left until they reached their quota, Billy and Mrs. Muller were feeling pretty good about themselves. Four victims down, and it wasn't even lunch time yet.

Adopting a stealthier approach, Matt took pride in his ability to get as close to his victims as possible before taking them out. In fact, sometimes he spent longer than necessary following them around, the thrill of remaining undetected second only to the delight he felt at the sudden look of terror in their eyes when they realized their number was up.

Meanwhile, Fiona and her team were functioning like a well-oiled assassination machine, with many of their victims surrendering once they realized escape was futile. Truth be known, some of their victims allowed themselves to be taken out on purpose, making it look like an accident in the hope of being grafted onto Fiona's team.

As the clandestine battle for top spot raged on, the rest of the town was also caught up in a frenzy of activity. Parade floats were being prepped, decorations were going up on Main Street, ball fields were being groomed, the high school cheerleading squad was practicing its routines, the marching band was going through a last-minute practice, and vintage cars, bikes, tractors, horses, and even pets were being decked out for the parade.

Meanwhile, a traveling midway had also arrived, the carnies busy setting up various rides, from bumper cars to a Ferris wheel. Even a fireworks crew had snuck into town overnight. Hired in secret by the Milligan Creek Daze committee, their surprise display would cap off the big day, the first time fireworks would factor in to a Milligan Creek Daze celebration.

By the end of the day, not only was the entire town giddy with excitement, in terms of the assassination game, only three teams remained: Fiona and her squad, Mrs. Muller and Billy, and Matt. Mrs. Muller and Billy had taken advantage of the Friday night preview of the midway to take out their fifth and final victim. The three of them had gone into the haunted house attraction, but only two of them, Mrs. Muller and Billy, had come out—dry, that is.

§

As darkness fell, Matt went through his usual routine of feigning tiredness, so he could go to bed early and then sneak out his window and find a safe place to sleep. But on that most important of nights, his parents' tolerance of his abnormal behavior finally hit a wall.

"Matt, before you go to bed, your father and I would like a word with you," Mrs. Taylor said.

Matt let out a sigh, his hand on the doorknob to his bedroom. "Can't it wait till tomorrow? I'm exhausted, and I have to get up early and—"

"We know what's going on, Matt," his mother said.

Matt's face flushed with fear. "You . . . you do?"

His mother nodded, patting the kitchen chair beside her. Matt reluctantly released his hold on the doorknob, sidled into the kitchen, and took a seat. He kept his eyes on the floor, afraid to look his parents in the eye.

"It's about that girl, isn't it?" Mrs. Taylor said.

Matt looked up at her. "What girl?"

"You know, Fickleberrybush," his father said.

"Pickleberrybush." Matt corrected him. "Fiona? What about her?"

"All this running," Mrs. Taylor said. "You're doing it for her, aren't you?"

Matt didn't know how to reply to that. In a way, he was, but in another way, he wasn't.

"And you and Chad, you used to be as thick as thieves, and now you hardly spend any time together," Mr. Taylor said. "If I didn't know better, I would say you're going out of your way to avoid each other. I hope you're not letting a girl come between you. Blood is thicker than water, you know."

Matt sniffed. "Tell that to Chad."

"It takes two to tango," his mother said. "If you and Chad are fighting over Fiona, you can't put all the blame on him—or her. You're responsible for your own actions."

Matt sighed. "I know."

They all looked up as they heard the front door open. It was Chad. When he saw Matt, he froze, half in and half out of the doorway. "Oh, sorry, if you're in the middle of—"

"No, you're exactly the person we want to see," Mrs. Taylor said. "Come in here. And while you're at it, take off those infernal sunglasses!"

Chad slid the sunglasses off as he edged into the room, letting the screen door slam shut behind him.

"We were just talking about Miss Pickleberrybush and how you and Matt have allowed her to come between you," Mr. Taylor said.

"Yeah, you know, it's why I'm doing all that *running*," Matt added, signaling to Chad that his parents had no idea what was really going on.

"It's not my fault," Chad replied. "Matt's had every opportunity to—"

"As we were just telling Matt, this isn't about placing blame," Mrs. Taylor said. "I don't know what's gotten into you two, but ever since we got back from BC, you've gone from best friends to worst enemies, and I want it to stop. Understand?"

"Yes, Mom," Chad said, hanging his head.

"I want you two to declare a truce," Mr. Taylor said. "Girls will come and go, but you'll always be brothers. Besides, you're too young for any of that romance stuff. You two should be out with your friends having fun, not obsessing over a girl. Dean I can understand, but I thought you two had more sense than that."

"We do," Chad protested, "but—"

"No buts," Mr. Taylor said. "I want you two to shake hands and be done with it. Got it?"

"Yes, Dad," Chad replied. He walked over to Matt and held out his hand. "Truce?"

Matt stared at Chad's hand in disgust, but a look from his mother told him he had better comply. "Truce." He shook Chad's hand, his other hand hidden beneath the table.

Mr. Taylor stood up. "Well, now that that's settled, let's see if I can still catch the last quarter of the Riders game on TV. Care to join me, boys?"

"Uh, I still need to get to bed early," Matt said. "What with Milligan Creek Daze happening tomorrow and all."

"Me too," Chad said, following Matt toward their bedroom. "Goodnight, Mom. Goodnight, Dad."

Their parents watched the boys, mystified. Then Mr. Taylor shrugged. "Guess we can't complain about a little alone time, can we, honey?" he said, putting his arm around his wife.

She gave him a squeeze. "You go turn on the TV. I'll get us some snacks."

By the time Chad made it into the bedroom, Matt was already halfway out the window.

"Wait!" Chad said. "I thought we declared a truce!"

"Ha!" Matt replied, sliding out the rest of the way and landing on the damp grass outside. "I had my fingers crossed on my other hand!"

"Wait a second anyway. I promise not to shoot you. You're not even our target."

Matt backed away from the window anyway until he was sure he was out of water pistol range, his ears tuned to the darkness in case Chad was merely trying to distract him as the other members of his team moved in. "Be quick about it," he said, grabbing a sleeping bag and a backpack from where he had hidden them in the bushes. "I've got a long hike ahead of me before I go to sleep tonight."

"That's the thing, Matt. You don't have to live your life on the run anymore. Just surrender and join our team. Then it'll be all of us against Mrs. Muller and Billy. Think about all the terrible things she's said and done to you over the years. It'll be your big chance to get her back—in public, no less."

136

Matt thought about it for a moment and then shook his head. "I'm sorry, Chad, but as tempting as that sounds, I only have one goal, the same goal I've had ever since she arrived in town: to teach Fiona Pickleberrybush a lesson."

Chad sighed. "You're never going to survive, Matt. You know that. Much less win."

"We'll see about that," Matt replied. "Cut off the head, and the snake will die. You'll see."

Chad shrugged. "It's your funeral." Then he held his thumb and index finger to his lips and blew a shrill whistle. "He's all yours, boys!"

Matt's eyes widened in shock. "What? But I thought—"

Chad smiled at his brother's distress. "When we shook hands, I was crossing my fingers too."

"You'll pay for this!" Matt growled. Then, with the sound of people crashing through the trees that surrounded the Taylors' farmyard drawing closer, Matt melted into the night.

19

THE PROTESTOR

Early the next morning, the recreation center parking lot northeast of Main Street was crammed with parade floats, classic cars, farming machinery, kids on decorated bikes, the high school marching band, a Ukrainian dancing troupe, senior citizens decked out in full Canadian Legion regalia, air cadets, the cheerleading squad, and pets dressed in ridiculous costumes. Even the town garbage truck had been adorned in streamers and ribbons for the occasion. The town's new bright red fire truck, which would carry Miss Milligan Creek, brought up the rear.

In the midst of the band tuning their instruments, the cheerleaders practicing their cheer, and the revving of engines, Otto, who had served as the parade marshal for the past three years, was running around with a clipboard in hand, shouting through his megaphone as he worked to ensure everything and everyone was in place prior to the parade getting underway.

At the front of the procession was a police car. Constable Link and Staff Sergeant Romanowski leaned against it as they waited for the signal to begin. Constable Link looked around, as if sniffing the air, and then shook his head. "I don't know, boss. I got a bad feeling about today, as if something big is going to happen. I still say we should have posted some extra security."

Staff Sergeant Romanowski looked askance at his young charge. "I think you've been watching way too much American TV."

"Maybe," Constable Link replied. "We'll see."

All along Main Street, people were lining up to watch the parade, some standing, some staking out a spot with lawn chairs, and others sitting on picnic blankets laid out along the curb.

If any of those people had looked up, they would have noticed a completely different type of preparation taking place on the flat rooftops of various downtown buildings. Having commandeered the area, Fiona's minions were busy setting up water balloon catapults, high-powered water guns, buckets full of wet sponges, garden hoses, and other weapons.

Andrew and Chad stood on rooftops on opposite sides of the street, scanning the crowd with binoculars, looking for any sign of Mrs. Muller, Billy, or Matt. They also had people interspersed amongst the crowd and on some of the floats, all of them keeping an eye out for their quarry.

Chad lowered his binoculars and held a walkie-talkie to his lips. "No sign of any of them yet. How about you, Andrew? Over."

"Negative," Andrew replied. "Over."

"Where could they be?" Chad asked. "Over."

"Don't worry; they'll show," Andrew said. "There's no way they would pass up this opportunity. Over and out."

Back at the parade marshaling grounds, Link and Romanowski were just about to get into their patrol car when a call came in over the radio. Romanowski reached inside and grabbed the CB microphone. "Romanowski here. Go ahead."

"Sir, we're getting complaints about a protestor down on Main Street."

Romanowski frowned. "A protestor. Who? And what are they protesting?"

"All I know is, it's an old woman," his dispatcher replied. "No one seems to recognize her. But she's holding a sign. She should be pretty easy to spot."

Romanowski checked his watch. They still had ten minutes before the parade was scheduled to begin. "Okay, we'll go check it out," he replied. "Romanowski out."

"Told you we should have hired extra security," Link said as he slid into the vehicle.

Romanowski scoffed. "I think the two of us are enough to handle one little old lady."

Farther back in the parade line-up, Henrietta Blunt adjusted the head on a Wetlands Unlimited mascot, a mallard duck, that was to march in front of the Milligan Creek Heritage Marsh float. Beside the mallard was a beaver mascot.

"It sure was kind of you to volunteer to represent the marsh, Mrs. Muller," Henrietta said as she pulled out a hairbrush and did some last-minute fixes on the beaver's fur.

"Shhhh!" Mrs. Muller said. "I don't want anyone to know it's me inside here!"

Henrietta smiled. "Of course! Virtue is its own reward, right? Wouldn't want to go trumpeting the fact you and Billy are sacrificing your time to represent the marsh in these no doubt hot, sweaty outfits when you could be enjoying the parade like everyone else. People might think you're bragging!"

"Exactly," Mrs. Muller said. "I appreciate your discretion in this matter."

Henrietta pretended to zip her lips. "Mum's the word!" Then she marched off to ensure the rest of her float was ready to go.

"Mrs. Muller, I don't know if I can make it through the entire parade wearing this," Billy said. "Did she have to use real beaver pelts to make this thing? It's boiling in here, and it stinks!"

"Keep it down!" Mrs. Muller said. "You want to blow our cover? I know it's hot—it's sweltering inside this duck suit too—but it's only for a short time, and it's going to be oh so worth it. Now zip it and remember what I taught you. The more you sweat in training . . ."

"The less you bleed in combat. I know, I get it," Billy replied. "But this isn't training. This is the real thing! Besides, I'm worried my sweat is going to soak my target."

"That's why I coated the back of it with wax paper!" Mrs. Muller replied.

"Yeah, but isn't it cheating to wear it inside our costumes instead of outside?"

"The rules clearly state that we have to wear them outside our *clothing*," Mrs. Muller pointed out. "And as far as I'm concerned, these costumes aren't clothing. They're made of animal skins and feathers. Now for the last time, keep quiet!"

It didn't take Link and Romanowski long to locate the protestor. Her sign, which said, "Arrest the Interloper!", was clearly visible above the crowd, the members of which were becoming increasingly agitated at her presence.

"Out of the way!" someone yelled.

"Yeah," another responded. "We can't see!"

"There's nothing to see!" the old woman replied in a creaky voice. "The parade hasn't even started yet, so pipe down back there!"

Tom Pew, who had been watching from a distance, elbowed Howard. "Hey, check out the new broad. Recognize her?"

Howard squinted in the old woman's direction and then shook his head. "Nope."

"Well, I think I'll go over and introduce myself," Tom said, taking off his tweed cap and going through the motion of smoothing his non-existent hair. "I like her spunk!"

Howard sniffed in disdain. "Have at it, Romeo."

Before Tom could make his move, Romanowski got out of his patrol car and approached the woman. "Hello, ma'am. What seems to be the problem here?"

"I'll tell you what the problem is," the old woman replied. "These people won't respect my right to protest."

Romanowski tilted his hat back slightly. "What exactly are you protesting?"

"Isn't it obvious? Miss Milligan Creek! There's no way that sunglass-wearing hussy should have won. She hasn't even lived here for more than a couple of months! Check the charter. There must be some kind of residency requirement."

Romanowski sighed and wiggled his mustache. He looked at the crowd. Everyone was watching him. He had to find a way to solve this problem, and quickly.

"Why did you wait until now to protest?" he asked. "The decision's already been made. It's too late to change anything now."

"Because I thought the community would come to its senses on their own. When they didn't, I decided to take matters into my own hands."

Romanowski took a deep breath and then let it out through his mouth. "Okay, you can protest, but you can't do it here. You need to stand back a bit, so you're not blocking anyone's view. Okay?"

"And take a chance Miss Trickleberrybush—"

"Pickleberrybush."

"Whatever! And take a chance she won't see my sign?

Forget it! I'm fully within my rights, and I plan to stay right here. If you want me to move, you'll have to arrest me. I'm sure that wouldn't be a problem for a big, strong man like you, arresting a little old woman in front of all these people, would it?"

Romanowski's mustache wiggled so much that it looked like a caterpillar had fallen out of a tree and landed on his upper lip. He knew the only way he could get the old woman to move would be to create an ugly scene. But if he allowed her to stay where she was, things could get even uglier.

Just when Romanowski was about to concede to the inevitable, Tom Pew stepped up, doffing his tweed hat at the protestor. "What seems to be the problem, officer?"

"The problem is these people won't respect my right to free speech!" the woman declared.

"Come on now," Romanowski said. "That's not really fair to—"

"Tell you what," Tom said, "why don't you come and stand by me? I've got a great view of the parade. You can even stand on the trunk of my car, so you won't be blocking anyone. "

He held out his arm for her. After a moment's hesitation, she slid her arm around his. "Well, it's nice to see chivalry isn't completely dead in this town," she said over her shoulder as Tom led her away.

Romanowski shook his head and then went back to his patrol car.

"Problem solved?" Link asked.

"I think so," Romanowski replied as he watched Tom lead the old woman into the crowd. He put the car into gear. "I hate to say it, but maybe you were right about that extra security detail."

20

MAN DOWN!

Finally, the big moment arrived. Otto blew his whistle, and the parade began its slow procession out of the parking lot, around the corner, and down Main Street.

As the cavalcade crawled along, Chad and Andrew continued to scan the crowd from their respective rooftops. "You still don't see them?" Dean asked, coming up beside Chad and craning his neck for a better look. He was manning a water balloon catapult on Chad's side of the street.

Chad shook his head slightly, still looking through the binoculars. "Nope."

"What could they be planning?" Dean wondered. "Maybe they won't show."

Chad lowered his binoculars and looked at Dean. "And miss out on the perfect opportunity to win the game in front of the entire town? Not a chance. Just be ready with the catapult. And if you see anything unusual, get on the horn." He held the binoculars to his eyes again and resumed his scrutiny of the crowd.

Down below, Tom beamed as he stood on the trunk of his car next to what he believed to be the prettiest woman in town. Making the moment even better, everyone could see him. Howard Long, eat your heart out!

"I really admire your pluckiness," Tom said. "I just wish there were more people like you who had the guts to speak truth to power and the sense to keep their ear to the ground." Suddenly, a thought occurred to him. "Excuse me, ma'am, but I don't believe I got your name."

The old woman blinked bashfully at him. "Names aren't important, honey. I'll tell you what though, could you do me a favor? Hold this for me." She handed him her sign. "I need to run to the little old ladies' room," she whispered, winking at him.

"Sure thing," Tom said as she hopped down off the trunk of his car, surprisingly spry for a woman her age. "But hurry back! You don't want to miss anything!"

Moments later, a member of Fiona's team, who was standing amongst the onlookers near Tom's car while scanning the crowd from behind his dark sunglasses, felt someone nudge him.

"Excuse me," he said. "I didn't mean to—"

Suddenly, he felt a peculiar sensation on his chest. He looked down. His target was soaked through!

Frantic, he looked around, but there was no sign of Matt, Mrs. Muller, or Billy. He raised his walkie-talkie to his lips. "Mayday, mayday! We have a man down!"

In front of the Milligan Creek Heritage Marsh float, which featured a beaver pond filled with real water, a beaver lodge and a dam made from real sticks, and stuffed beavers, on loan from a local taxidermist, Billy struggled to keep up with Mrs. Muller. As he trudged along in his beaver suit, which was becoming increasingly weighed down with sweat, Mrs. Muller waved merrily to the crowd while tugging his arm.

"C'mon, Billy, keep up!" she hissed. "And keep an eye out for Matt. He could be anywhere in this crowd."

"I can't see anything from inside this stupid costume,"

Billy complained, trying to adjust the beaver's head. "Besides, it's like a sauna in here."

In the crowd, the members of Fiona's crew continued to drop like flies. The same pattern kept repeating itself, each person feeling someone bump into them, only to emerge from the encounter with the front of their shirt soaking wet. The walkie-talkies were going crazy with reports of one death after another.

"We're getting slaughtered out there," Chad said. "But how, and by who? That does it." He handed his binoculars to Dean. "I'm going to go down there and find out."

Still clutching the old woman's sign, Tom perused the crowd, waiting impatiently for her to return.

"Can you put that thing down, please?" a woman behind him asked. "My kids and I are trying to watch a parade here."

"Oh, sorry," Tom said, lowering the sign. He wished he had even half the old woman's boldness.

Even Mrs. Muller was beginning to lose her cool as she trudged along. None of the children who waved at the duck mascot would have guessed at the scowling woman behind its smiling face.

"Where could that Taylor boy be?" she grumbled.

At that moment, a commotion in the crowd drew her eye. A kid in black sunglasses held his hands in the air as he looked down at the front of his shirt, which was soaking wet. "Dang it, I'm out! Who did that?"

As he looked around for his assailant, Mrs. Muller's eyes flicked over the crowd. The perpetrator, he or she had to be nearby. She spotted a figure hurrying away through the masses. It didn't look like Matt though. The person had gray hair pulled back into a bun, a cane, and . . . a water pistol, which Mrs. Muller saw her tuck under her shawl! That was no old woman. That was . . .

"Matt Taylor!" Mrs. Muller exclaimed, pulling a huge water gun out from beneath her mallard costume. "Prepare to meet your maker!"

"Mommy! Mommy!" a little girl screamed, pointing at the mascot. "That ducky has a gun!"

Pandemonium broke out as people screamed and shoved each other out of the way, inadvertently opening up a clear path between Mrs. Muller and Matt, whose wig was knocked off in the tumult, smearing his carefully applied makeup. He tried to get away, but the crowd blocked his escape on every side.

Mrs. Muller ripped the head off her duck costume, causing the audience to let out another scream. Then she wiped her sweaty hair out of her eyes, making her look a bit more human. "Any last words, punk?" she asked, pointing her gun at Matt.

"Yeah, any last words, punk?" Billy said as he bumped into Mrs. Muller, blinded by sweat and the poor eyeholes in his mask. The costume also muffled his voice, so all anyone else heard was, "Hany hast herds, hunk?"

"Yeah, I do," Matt replied, confidence returning to his face. "Look out behind you."

Mrs. Muller scoffed, surprisingly cool despite the chaos unfolding around her. "Oldest trick in the—"

At that moment, Henrietta, who had been throwing educational wetlands pamphlets wrapped around candy and waving to the crowd, realized her mascots had stopped moving, and the float was about to run them over. "Brake!" she yelled to her driver. "Brake!"

He slammed on the brakes, bringing the float to a skidding stop. The water in the beaver pond, however, kept moving, overflowing the dam and washing right over Mrs. Muller and Billy, the force of it knocking them flat onto their faces on the pavement.

21

"I Don't Know What Came Over Me."

"Mrs. Muller is down! I repeat, Mrs. Muller is down!" Andrew yelled into his walkie-talkie as he watched the action unfold through his binoculars. "Matt Taylor is the new target. I repeat, Matt Taylor. All units, open fire!"

Up and down Main Street, on every rooftop, the catapult, sponge, and garden hose crews had finally received the news they'd been waiting for. They launched a barrage of projectiles and streams of water down on the unsuspecting crowd, adopting a "spray and pray" approach in the hope of somehow soaking Matt in the process. Startled by the surprise bombardment, the crowd of onlookers turned into a panicked mass of mindless automatons, driven by fear.

At the front of the parade, Romanowski and Link were waving at the crowd when their police radio crackled to life. "Sir, we've got a report of a duck with a gun."

Link and Romanowski looked at each other. "Come again?" Romanowski said, keying his mic.

"Sorry, staff sergeant, a duck mascot, and it appears to be a water gun. Apparently, a beaver is involved in the incident as well."

"Is the beaver armed too?" Romanowski asked sarcastically, grinning at Constable Link.

"Affirmative," the dispatcher replied. "But both were taken out by the Milligan Creek Heritage Marsh float."

"Oh my gosh, that's Henrietta's float," Romanowski exclaimed. He and Henrietta had been an item for a few months now, ever since the radio incident at the marsh. He keyed the mic again. "Is Henri—is everyone okay?"

"Yes, sir," his dispatcher replied, "but I suggest you get back there and take a look. Pandemonium appears to have broken out. As soon as the duck and the beaver went down, water started bombarding the crowd from everywhere."

Without hesitation, Romanowski turned on the car's lights and siren and turned left down a side street. The crowd cheered, thinking it was all part of the show. The water bombardment had yet to reach their part of the parade.

His cover blown, Matt shed the rest of his disguise and ran toward the rear of the parade, water balloons exploding all around him. In all likelihood, he was about to go down, but not if he could get to Fiona first. He wove in and out of floats, dodging horses and pets and crouching behind classic cars and farm machinery to shield himself.

As Matt ran past the Milligan Creek historical society's float, a kid wearing black sunglasses popped out of a replica log cabin and jumped down in front of him, his gun drawn, but Matt shot the kid before he had a chance to squeeze the trigger. That's when Matt noticed the water supply in his own gun was dangerously low.

Desperate for a refill, he spotted the aquatic center's float just ahead. It featured Waldo lifting weights and Lance pretending to be an overly protective lifeguard, shouting through a megaphone at a group of kids enjoying themselves in a hot tub. Without a second thought, Matt clambered aboard.

"Sorry, folks. This'll just take a minute," Matt said as he

submerged his water pistol in the hot tub.

"Hey, that's our water!" Lance cried. He raised his megaphone to his lips. "Waldo, that kid's stealing our water! Get him!"

Waldo finished his final rep, pausing to nod at a couple of teenage girls who gasped at his bulging biceps, and then dropped his dumbbells and pointed a threatening finger at Matt. "Get off our float, you little punk!" Before the musclebound oaf could grab him, Matt jumped off the float and ran away.

As he raced down the street, he dodged not only projectiles fired from the rooftops but also water sprinklers, kids racing past doing drive-by shootings on their bikes, a blast of water gushing out of a fire hydrant that someone had opened up, and even a couple of dogs with remote-controlled water guns mounted on their backs.

Finally, he spotted it: the fire truck. On top of it was Fiona. She was decked out in a prom dress, a tiara, a shiny white satin "Miss Milligan Creek" sash, and her signature sunglasses and headphones as she smiled and waved at the crowd. Her target was pinned to her sash.

"Fiona, over here!" Mayor Bondar called, snapping her picture when she turned to him and posed, smiling brightly. Then he stood on his tiptoes, his eyes searching the crowd. "I sure hope one of Otto's reporters is getting this."

Fiona was so far back in the parade and so distracted by her duties as Miss Milligan Creek that she still had no idea about the chaos that was unfolding up front. Perfect.

Matt looked back and saw a mob of sunglass-wearing assassins closing in. He knew he would only get one shot at this, so he had to make it count. Doubling his efforts, he raced straight for the fire truck.

Luckily for him, Fiona was looking the other way as he ran up to the front of the truck—at least she appeared to be looking the other way. That was one advantage of wearing sunglasses all the time: no one could see her eyes. And at that moment, even though she appeared to be looking away, her eyes were focused on Matt.

Not only did Matt fail to realize that Fiona was looking at him, he also couldn't have known that, earlier that morning, Fiona had charmed one of the younger firemen into giving her a quick tutorial on how the fire truck's water cannon worked. In the process, he happened to mention that the truck's water tank was always kept full, just in case of emergency. In Fiona's mind, if any moment counted as an emergency, this was it.

"Excuse me," Fiona said, touching the young fireman's arm, "but would you mind getting me my water bottle? I'm feeling a bit faint in this heat."

"Why certainly," he replied, eager to impress the beautiful young woman.

The moment he turned his back, Fiona gripped the handles on the water cannon. "Hey, Matt Taylor!" she yelled. "Prepare to get your hair wet!"

Before anyone could stop her, she flicked off the safety, and pulled the trigger.

§

Staff Sergeant Romanowski squealed the tires as the police cruiser rounded the corner, trying to find a place to cut in near the middle of the parade.

"Staff Sergeant Romanowski, this is dispatch. We now have a report of a princess firing a water cannon at the rear of the parade, over."

"A princess firing a what?" Romanowski cried.

"I told you we should have called in back-up," Link said, giving his superior a knowing look.

152

Romanowski glared at him, his mustache bristling. "Will you shut up!" He hit the brakes, backed up, and then turned down a back alley, this time racing toward the rear of the parade.

§

The moment Fiona pulled the trigger, Matt hit the pavement. The stream of water shot right over his head and slammed into the float that was directly in front of the fire truck. It was the float created by Abigail's beauty salon, on which she and Thelma were doing live makeovers while Abigail narrated their progress over a loudspeaker. They had just spun their client's chair around to show off the transformation when the blast of water hit. Not only did it obliterate all their hard work, it soaked Abigail and Thelma to the skin.

Otto, who happened to be walking alongside Abigail's float at the time, reacted exactly as anyone would expect the parade marshal to respond: with shock and indignation.

"This is outrageous!" he yelled, casting his eyes about to see who would dare to hose down Abigail's float. However, when he saw it was Fiona, anyone watching his face closely would have detected the ghost of a smile haunting his lips.

"Dye another day, Otto, get it?" Kelvin said, tapping him on the shoulder. "I said 'die', but in my mind, I spelled it d-y-e. That's what you call hairdresser humor."

Otto was thankful for the opportunity to laugh. "On any other day, Kelvin, that wouldn't be funny. But today? Today, it's hilarious." They did a high five.

Abigail broke down in tears, her mascara causing dark streaks to run down her cheeks, her lank hair sticking to the sides of her face. Then her eyes bristled with rage.

"Who did that? Who did that?"

She turned around, and her eyes settled on Fiona. "You! I knew you were the worst thing ever to happen to this town!"

She charged, apparently planning to leap off the float, climb onto the fire truck, and attack Fiona, but Thelma held her back.

"No, don't do it, Abigail!" Thelma cried. "Think of your fingernails! Your fingernails!"

Unable to control the powerful water cannon, and not thinking to pull her finger off the trigger, Fiona spun with it as it swept over the crowd, though she fought to send the water over their heads rather than risk hosing down the members of her own team, some of whom had already been caught in the crossfire.

"What the heck are you doing?" the young fireman yelled, clambering back up and pulling her hands off the trigger, reducing the torrent of water to a trickle.

"I'm sorry. I don't know what came over me," Fiona said. "Now if you'll excuse me . . .." She pulled a water gun out from under her Miss Milligan Creek sash. "I have a job to finish."

The fireman looked on in wonder and confusion as she clambered down from the fire truck and hightailed it after the mob of sunglass-wearing kids, who were racing down the street after Matt. Seizing the moment, he had doubled back toward the front of the parade while his pursuers shielded themselves from the water cannon.

The moment she was gone, Romanowski and Link screeched to a halt at the rear of the parade and jumped out of their car. "Where's the princess?" Romanowski asked.

"She went that way!" the fireman said, pointing toward the front of the parade. Romanowski pounded the roof of his patrol car. "You've got to be kidding me!"

22

POOL PARTY

Matt's lungs burned as he sprinted across Main Street and into the town's central park. He thought about hiding behind the war memorial, but when he looked back, Fiona's army was too close. Someone would be sure to see him. Then he saw the water tower looming before him, its new paint job gleaming in the July sun. Suddenly, he got an idea.

Veering away from the water tower, Matt ran straight toward the pool, which was located in the same park as the water tower, just a couple hundred feet away. Clambering over the chain-link fence, which was threaded with privacy strips on that side at the request of the seniors' aquasize class, he dropped down onto the pool deck and then raced toward the change rooms.

A moment later, Fiona's minions streamed over the fence like a herd of unrelenting army ants. Once inside the pool area, they stopped short, seeing no sign of Matt.

"Spread out!" Andrew said. "Look under the bleachers, in the shower rooms, and in the equipment room. He's got to be in here somewhere."

In a flash of white chiffon, Fiona herself dropped down over the fence. "Got him yet?"

"No," Andrew replied. "But we will."

"If at all possible, save him for me!" she said.

Andrew turned to face the others. "You heard the lady. Capture him, but don't shoot him!"

Seeking to get a better vantage point on the situation, Fiona climbed the ladder to the top of the high diving board. But even from up there, she couldn't spot him. "Where the heck could he have gone?" she asked.

Before the words were out of her mouth, she heard the whirring of an electric motor. It was followed by the emergence of a strange contraption over the roof of the pool office and change rooms—the boom lift that the painters had been using to repaint the water tower. Apparently, the pool building was next on their list. In the lift was Matt, and in his hands was a fire hose, the same one that he had attempted to spray Fiona with just a few days earlier.

"Looks like the tables have turned, Pickleberrybush," Matt said. He maneuvered the lift until it was out over the deep end of the pool, and he was level with her on the high diving board, though he was careful to stay just out of range of her water pistol. "Any final words?"

Fiona thought about it for a minute and then nodded, realizing she was beat. "Yes, actually." She set her water pistol down on the diving board. Then she removed her Walkman headphones and her sunglasses. "Before you shoot me, I think there's something you should know. There's a good reason why I didn't want to go in the water when I first got to town."

"Oh yeah?" Matt said. "And what's that?"

"This." No sooner were the words out of her mouth when she reached up . . . and pulled off her hair!

A gasp rippled through the crowd. Later reports said that some people fainted, including some boys, but none of those accounts could be confirmed.

"You're . . . bald?" Matt said, as surprised as everyone else. "But why? And why didn't you tell anyone?"

To everyone's surprise, Fiona started to tear up. "All my life, I had long, flowing, raven-black hair, and then one morning, I woke up, and it had all fallen out, and it's never grown back! Even my eyebrow hair fell out, which is why I wear sunglasses. The kids in my old town teased me relentlessly, and I was afraid the same thing would happen here if people found out. I was afraid no one would like me. I was afraid *you* wouldn't like me."

"Me?" Matt replied, stupefied. "Why would you care about me? Why did you think . . . wait a second, me? But I thought . . . but you . . .."

"Yo, dummy, I think she's trying to say she likes you," Chad said.

"Awwwwww . . .," practically all the girls chorused at once, caught up in the romance of the moment.

Matt stared at Fiona, his face a mask of confusion as his brain struggled to compute everything that had happened over the past few days.

"I hate to be a wet blanket here, but we're still in the midst of the game," Andrew said, "and we've yet to declare a winner."

"That's right," Chad said. "Take up your positions, people. Catapulters, prepare to fire at my command!"

"And somebody find the faucet to turn off that fire hose!" Andrew added.

As Matt watched Fiona's army scurry around while preparing to fire anything and everything that might be able to hit him up in the boom lift, he knew it was now or never. But after what Fiona had just confessed to him and the rest of the kids, did he really have the heart to take her out?

Sensing his distress, Fiona took a few steps back on the diving board. "Don't worry, Matt, I'll make it easy for you."

"No, Fiona, don't do it!" Dean yelled. "Don't make the same mistake I—"

But it was too late. Raising her arms over her head like an Olympic diver, she took one quick step forward with her left foot, drove her right knee up, came down hard on two feet, and launched herself into the air, prom dress and all.

The crowd oohed and aahed in wonder as her body arced gracefully through the air, doing a perfect swan dive. For many of them, it was the strangest and yet most beautiful thing they had ever seen. A second later, she disappeared below the water's surface with hardly a splash. The crowd erupted into cheers.

"You won, Matt!" Chad said. "Congratulations!"

Despite having lost to Matt, the rest of the players couldn't help but cheer as well. But their celebration was interrupted by a voice calling from outside the fence. "Wait, wait, I'm still in! I'm still in!"

Before anyone could react, Mrs. Muller pulled herself over the fence and then flopped down onto the pool deck, her puffy mascot costume cushioning her fall. Billy was right behind her, still wearing his beaver suit. Her costume cushioned his fall as well.

Mrs. Muller wasted no time scrambling to her feet, brandishing her water gun. "I'm still in the game!" she repeated, holding up her target, which was still unharmed. "Thankfully, Henrietta thought to make this costume out of real duck feathers, and, as the saying goes, that little beaver pond mishap was like water off a duck's back."

"And off a beaver's fur," Billy added, but all anyone heard through his mask was, "Unt rof a peaver's tur."

"I'm confused," Chad said. "Does this mean we're all on Matt's side?" All the weapons in the place turned on Mrs. Muller.

"Now hold on just a second," Mrs. Muller said as she and Billy backed up toward the fence.

"Or does it mean we're on Mrs. Muller's side?" Chad continued, causing all the weapons to turn back toward Matt. Chad looked at Andrew, who was always good at helping them think their way out of difficult situations. "What do you think, Andrew?"

"Well, technically speaking, Mrs. Muller killed her last victim *before* Matt killed—before Fiona took herself out. Therefore, it would appear that we're all on Mrs. Muller's side—that is, if she wants to go that route and bring us all onto her team."

"Are you crazy?" Mrs. Muller asked. "Of course you're all on my team. So, stop standing there like a bunch of numbskulls, and open fire."

"You heard the woman," Billy said. "Ready, aim . . .."

Before Billy could utter his last command, Matt climbed over the protective railing of the boom lift, looked down at where Fiona was treading water in the deep end, peering up at him, and jumped.

As he sailed through the air, water balloons and sponges and streams of water shot past him, but not one of them hit him before he struck the water with a mighty splash.

"I won!" Mrs. Muller exclaimed, linking arms with Billy and spinning him around in a circle. "I won the game!"

"We won," Billy reminded her.

At that moment, they heard a siren approach. As if on cue, kids started scrambling over the fence, hoping to escape before the police arrived.

"Oh boy," Dean said. "We're going to have a lot of explaining to do."

"That can wait," Chad said. "Come on!" Without a moment's hesitation, he jumped into the pool.

"Aw, why not?" Dean said. "For once, my mom won't

be the one giving me heck. Whoo-hoo!" He did a cannon-ball into the water. Many of the other kids who had been climbing the fence to escape paused. It was a hot day, and the police couldn't throw them all in jail, could they?

As the water exploded with kids doing cannonballs, can openers, and Schmitters, Matt surfaced in the deep end and noticed something floating in the water. He grabbed it and swam over to Fiona. "Here," he said. "You may want this."

Fiona looked at her wig, which had fallen off the diving board when she jumped. It was a sopping wet mess. "Do you think I need it?"

Matt thought about it for a moment and then smiled. "Not at all."

She grinned back. "Then neither do I." She grabbed the wig out of Matt's hand and tossed it aside.

Everybody cheered—even Mrs. Muller.

At that moment, the gate to the pool flew open, revealing Staff Sergeant Romanowski and Constable Link. "Alright, nobody move!" Romanowski yelled. "This is the police!"

23

THE BIG DATE

One week later, the town of Milligan Creek had been restored to normal—almost.

When the parents discovered what their children had been up to over the past several days, some of them were furious. But they weren't nearly as angry that their kids had been running around town trying to assassinate each other as they were about the disruption of the town's biggest annual event. Thankfully, once Otto, Staff Sergeant Romanowski, Constable Link, and a group of volunteers restored order, the rest of the parade went off without a hitch, as did the other Milligan Creek Daze events. And everyone agreed that the fireworks display would have to become an annual tradition.

In a hastily called emergency meeting of the Miss Milligan Creek committee, a minimum residency requirement of twelve months was added to the list of rules, satisfying Abigail as well as her daughter, Natalie, who was crowned Miss Milligan Creek after Fiona was defrocked due to "behavior unbecoming her position," as Otto put it in the paper, even though writing those words went against every fiber of his being. If it had been his choice, he would have given Fiona a medal.

As for Tom, he was still heartsick over having loved and lost the little old lady, whose name he never did get. He decided to keep her protest sign as a memento, hoping that one day she might return for it, like Cinderella and her glass slipper. He didn't realize he had that story backwards, that it should be him looking for her, not her looking for him, but it comforted him nonetheless. He was also convinced the woman's sudden disappearance was the work of vast conspiracy, and he was determined to get to the bottom of it, even if it took the rest of his days.

Ben remained angry at Emily for betraying him—twice. But, being a resourceful girl, she figured out the perfect way to make peace: by giving him half of her candy stash.

"Moo," Ben said in response. In his language, that meant, "Thank you."

Dean went out of his way to avoid the Co-op for a while, for fear of running into Darcy and Patrick, but thankfully for Darcy, Gwen didn't. With her mom laid up with a broken leg, Pam, accompanied by Gwen, had to do most of the shopping. That provided plenty of opportunities for Darcy to become Gwen's "personal shopper." Eventually, she agreed to go on a double date with him and Pam and Patrick to see a movie. It was a start.

Staff Sergeant Romanowski received the surprise of his life the Monday after the parade when Constable Link informed him he had applied for a transfer.

"What?" Romanowski exclaimed. "You haven't even been here for a month!"

"I know," Link replied, "but I'm not sure I can handle the stress of a place like this."

"Where are you planning to go?" Romanowski asked.

"I don't know, Vancouver, Winnipeg, Regina, Toronto, any place but here."

§

As the sun headed toward the horizon the following Saturday evening, Matt and his family drove toward the Mullers' house. While the rest of the family wore casual clothes, Matt was dressed in a suit and tie, and he had even allowed Joyce to put some styling gel into his hair. He was also holding a bouquet of flowers.

"Would you stop messing with it?" Matt said, slapping Joyce's hand away from his head. She, Matt, and Chad were crammed in the back seat of the family's station wagon.

"You only get one chance to make a first impression," she replied.

Matt rolled his eyes. "I think it's way too late for that with Mrs. Muller."

"I still can't believe you're going through with it," Chad replied. "A date with Dean's mom." He shook his head. "Wow. I hate to admit it, but you've got *way* more guts than I do."

"He doesn't have a choice," Joyce said. "A rule's a rule."

"Don't worry, Matt, you'll do just fine," Mrs. Taylor assured him.

"Just remember to compliment her on how good she looks," Mr. Taylor reminded him. "Works every time."

"It does, does it?" Mrs. Taylor smiled as she elbowed her husband in the ribs.

"Hey, don't distract the driver!" Mr. Taylor replied with a grin.

Finally, the station wagon came to a stop outside the Mullers' house.

"Break a leg, kid," Joyce said.

"Not if she breaks yours first!" Chad quipped. He and Joyce did a high five.

"Thanks," Matt muttered. "For nothing."

Taking a deep breath, he got out of the car. Then he walked up the front steps and rang the doorbell. Moments later, Mrs. Muller, also dressed to the nines, opened the door.

"Well, well, well, Matt Taylor. I hardly recognized you without that infernal Oilers cap. And your hair. It looks . . . different." She looked like she was about to say something more, but then she shook her head. "Anyway, come in, come in." She stepped aside, so he could enter.

"Are you . . . are you sure Mr. Muller is alright with this?" Matt asked.

"Alright with it? It was his idea," she replied. "Now come on; you don't want the food to get cold."

Matt entered the Mullers' dining room and then stopped dead in his tracks. "What's she—what're you doing here, Fiona?"

She smiled at him, resplendent in a new dress as she sat at the end of the Mullers' dining room table. No headphones, no sunglasses, and no hair! (Although she had lightly penciled in some eyebrows.) As Matt fought to regain his composure, he noticed the table was set for two, including a white lace tablecloth with matching napkins and Audrey's finest bone china, crystal, and silverware.

"Don't just stand there like a dork; have a seat," Mrs. Muller said, pulling out a chair that was kitty corner to Fiona and practically shoving Matt into it.

In shock, Matt suddenly realized he was still holding the bouquet. "I . . . I guess these are for you," he said, handing them to Fiona.

"Boy, do you ever need to work on your sweet talking," Mrs. Muller said as she disappeared into the kitchen. "I guess these are for you? Ha!"

Fiona smiled as she accepted the flowers. "Thanks, Matt. They're beautiful."

Matt reddened slightly. "So, how long have you known about this?"

"A couple of days. Mrs. Muller felt bad about her win, considering she never should have been playing the game in the first place, not to mention hiding her and Billy's targets under their costumes. She thought this would be a good way to make it up to both of us."

"Wow, she really must have hit her head when she flopped over that fence," Matt said. "It almost sounds like you're saying she wanted to be nice."

Fiona grinned. A moment later, Dean emerged from the kitchen wearing a black tie and a white shirt. He had a towel draped over one arm, and he was holding a tray in the other. "Your cocktails, mademoiselle and monsieur," he said in his best French accent.

"Merci," Matt replied. "So, you're all in on this."

"Not because I want to be," Dean whispered as Billy entered with a tray of hors-d'œuvres—spring rolls, in keeping with Fiona's request for Chinese food. "But if I do a good job, Mom promised to cut me in on the prize money."

"Her share only," Billy reminded him.

Dean clenched his teeth in frustration. "I know. For the *tenth* time."

"I'll be sure to give you a good review," Matt whispered, chuckling.

Dean grinned. "Thanks. By the way, nice hair."

Matt smiled self-consciously as he reached up and touched it. "Thanks."

Once Dean and Billy went back into the kitchen, Matt and Fiona looked into each other's eyes and grinned sheepishly, both of them unsure of what to say. Finally, Fiona raised her glass. "To good friends."

Matt thought for a second and then raised his glass in response. "And even better enemies." They both laughed as they clinked glasses and then took a sip.

"Ah, sparkling water," Matt said, smacking his lips. "How appropriate." Then he held out his glass to her, his face somber. "Welcome to Milligan Creek, Fiona Pickleberrybush. Seriously."

Fiona smiled, her eyes glistening. "Thanks."

Matt set his glass down and cleared his throat. "Before this date goes any further, I think there's something you should know."

"Oh yeah? What's that?"

"This."

Back in the kitchen, Mr. Muller tapped his wife on the shoulder as she peeked out the door at the two young lovebirds. "Hey, haven't you done enough skulking around for one summer?"

When she turned around, her eyes were wet with tears. "He shaved his head! He shaved his head, so Fiona wouldn't feel bad about being bald!"

Mr. Muller peeked out just in time to see Matt set his "hair" on the table.

"I made it out of your wig," Matt said. "I was going to show you later, but I figured now is as good a time as any. I hope you don't mind," he said, running his hand over his bare scalp.

"Mind?" Fiona asked, tears of joy running down her cheeks. "I love it!"

She reached across the table and gave him a hug.

Mr. Muller sniffled and wiped his nose as he eased back from the doorway and turned toward his wife. "I always told you Matt was a good kid."

She scoffed as she dabbed the tears from her eyes. "I never said he wasn't!"

"But you're always so hard on him."

"Only because I know he can take it."

166

Mr. Muller put his arm around her as the two of them peeked out at Matt and Fiona. "Is that why you're so hard on me and Dean, because we're so tough?"

Mrs. Muller glanced back at her son, who was standing by Billy as the two of them waited to serve the main course. "I don't know," she said. "Maybe after supper I should run the two of you through my obstacle course, and we'll see just how tough you are. What do you say, Billy?"

Billy crossed his arms over his chest and grinned. "Yes, sir—er, ma'am. Excellent idea."

"No way!" Dean said, holding up his hands and backing away from his mother. "No way!"

His parents laughed and then turned back to spy on the young couple.

"Go ahead, make my day." A rubber tipped take-off from Clint Eastwood would be appropriate for Rick Larson, a competitor in the Assassins game that hit the city for two weeks. It finished Sunday, with 44 dead.
—Enterprise Photo

Spy vs Spy: you can shoot or die

By Lindsey Galloway
Enterprise Staff

The boards can come off the windows. It's safe to walk the streets of Yorkton again.

The Assassin Game is over and 44 of the city's finest prospective recruits for Canada's new secret spy network have been killed.

The deadly tales were suspiciously similar:

As the final factory whistles blow and the sun begins to set, a slight movement is detected in the shadows. A head turns suddenly as footsteps approach and the chase is on ... a life and death battle on Betts Avenue. In the end, only one walks away.

Fortunately, it was murder without bloodshed. The assassin game is played with suction cup pistols, although some of the players clearly utilized some innate killer instinct.

Two Yorkton residents organized the "kill for fun" game to break the "monotony of the summer months."

"It's like playing cops and robbers, but a little more real," said organizer Rick Larson, who started the game with his brother Glenn.

For one week, the 46 competitors stalked the streets, tracking their victims, all the while wary that an unknown killer was on their tail.

The rules for the game, which Larson hopes becomes an annual event, are simple. Players are given an information package about their victim, including a picture, home address and work address. One cannot be killed while working. A hit anywhere on the body is a kill.

Cunning and caution are the major assets in playing the game. The weak are eliminated quick.

"My brother and I were delivering the cards and didn't get home until 12:10 and the game started at midnight and somebody was already waiting for me. But I outfoxed him and he chased me through the neighbourhood for quite a while. He didn't get me until almost two o'clock.

"When he was chasing me, I felt like Lee Harvey Oswald," Larson said, adding that some players camped out with friends to avoid similar traps.

The successful killer goes on to hunt the player listed on his victim's card.

Larson said the killer instinct is often ingenius.

"One guy used car trouble as a ploy. He pulled up in front of his victim's house and managed to get the father to come out and give him a boost. Then they got to talking and the assassin mentioned that he happened to know the man's son. The man said, 'Yeah, he's in the kitchen right now', the assassin pulled out his gun, sprinted into the house and killed the son," he said, adding his brother was killed in his sleep when an assassin-friend found the spare key to his house and snuck down to the basement where he slept.

By Friday, the numbers had dwindled to just two. Lyndon Surjik needed only to stay alive until the Sunday noon deadline to win by virtue of his superior number of kills. Cam Kock needed the kill. Although Surjik made some attempts, dressed in drag, to track down his opponent, who was also tracking his elusive enemy.

Koch later managed to gain entrance to Surjik's house, hidden in a box delivered by friends as a dishwasher for the family. Once inside, he sprang out of the box, and in the resulting confusion, shot Surjik's brother, allowing Lyndon to find refuge in the bathroom. Surjik's cautious strategy won out over Koch's cunning.

But next year Kock will be a year older and a year wiser.

Yorkton may never be the same.

168

A Brief Note on the Inspiration Behind This Book

This novel wouldn't have been possible without three things. The first is the newspaper article on the facing page, which I clipped from the *Yorkton Enterprise* way back in 1984 (when I was in grade eight). Inspired by the story, I had planned to play Assassin with my friends, but I never quite pulled it together. Then last summer while driving home from a family holiday, my wife, Heidi; my eldest daughter, Gretchen; and I came up with the rules for a new version of Assassin. It was inspired in no small part by the video game Destiny, which my youngest son, Zeph, had introduced to me a few years earlier. We tested our version at my eldest son Huw's birthday party, ironed out a few kinks, and that game became the centerpiece for this book.

Making the genesis of this novel a true family affair, the second element that made this novel possible came from my youngest daughter, Lark. One day we were joking about funny names when she came up with the last name "Pickleberrybush." I liked the sound of it and said I should use it in one of my next books. Lark said that was fine, but if I did, the girl's first name had to be "Fiona."

That moment was a breakthrough for me, because until that point, I had been thinking about building *The Water War* around some criminals who hide out in Milligan Creek right when the Assassin game breaks out, only to think they've stumbled upon some real-life assassins, who are after them. Real crime gets mixed up with the make-believe game, chaos ensues, and in the end, a winner is declared and a crime is solved. While I thought the idea had some merit, it felt like it veered too far toward the Hardy Boys (a series that I love but which I do not wish to emulate). The minute Lark uttered the words, "Fiona Pickleberrybush," I knew exactly which direction I wanted to go instead.

Finally, we have *American Ninja Warrior*. Yes, you heard that right. Everyone in our family loves the show (especially co-host Akbar Gbaja-Biamila's wild reactions). One competitor in particular inspired Fiona's big reveal on the high diving board at the end of this novel: Kevin Bull. Kevin is not only an amazing athlete, he is also affected by alopecia totalis, an autoimmune disease that causes all the hair on a person's scalp and body to fall out. This can be emotionally devastating to those affected. However, rather than wallow in self-pity, Kevin volunteers his time to inspire and support young people who share his condition through the Children's Alopecia Project (https://www.childrensalopeciaproject.org/). I hope this novel also inspires those affected by the alopecia to "let their wig fly."

All that to say, one of the best things about writing is that you never know when or where inspiration will strike. But when it does, pounce on it, and hold onto it, even if you have to wait thirty-four (!) years before it pays off.

About the Author

Kevin Miller grew up on a farm outside of Foam Lake, Saskatchewan, where he dreamed of becoming a writer. He got his first break as a newspaper reporter in Meadow Lake, SK. Within a year, he parlayed that into a job in book publishing, which eventually enabled him to become a full-time freelance writer and editor.

From there, Kevin transitioned into film, and he spent the next thirteen years traveling the world while working on a variety of feature films, documentaries, and short film projects. In addition to serving as a writer, he has also worked as a director, producer, and film editor.

These days, Kevin splits his time between writing, editing, filmmaking, and teaching. When he's not working, he enjoys hanging out with his wife and four kids, fishing, hiking, canoeing, skiing, playing hockey, skateboarding, and otherwise exploring his world.

Kevin likes to talk about books, movies, and writing almost as much as he enjoys writing. If you'd like to contact Kevin about any of these topics, to tell him what you think of his novels, or to book him for a speaking engagement, you can reach him at www.kevinmillerxi.com.

UP THE CREEK!

When best friends Matt, Chad, Dean, and Andrew set out on a canoe trip down Milligan Creek during spring run-off season, little do they realize that their voyage through small-town Saskatchewan is about to turn into one of the wildest experiences of their lives—if they survive!

UNLIMITED

A school field trip to the local Wetlands Unlimited marsh just outside of Milligan Creek, SK, gives Matt, Chad, Dean, and Andrew a brilliant idea: hijacking the radio signal that transmits a recorded message about the marsh and using it to launch their own pirate radio station. Broadcasting late at night, mostly for their own amusement, their show quickly becomes an underground sensation. Keeping their identities a secret, the boys are ecstatic about the growing popularity of their program, until it draws the attention of Wetlands Unlimited—and the police!

COMING SOON

THE GREAT GRAIN ELEVATOR INCIDENT

When Milligan Creek's iconic grain elevators are slated for demolition, to be replaced by a huge, ugly inland grain terminal a couple of miles from town, Matt, Chad, Andrew, and Dean concoct a wild scheme to save their grain elevators—and their small prairie community—from being wiped off the face of the planet.

For more details, visit www.millstonepress.ca.